THE BRIDE RUNS AWAY

"It was the most fortunate thing I have ever done! Here you are and I have just enjoyed a meal more than I have ever enjoyed one before and I recognised the Parisian touch at every scintillating mouthful."

Then the Earl said in a very different tone,

"I only hope you are staying. But I will be honest and tell you, as I am sure you have been told already, that I cannot pay you for working for me."

"That I understand, my Lord. I would be glad to stay for reasons I don't wish to discuss at present, while I make up my mind where I will go next."

The Earl stared at her and then he said,

"I have the strangest feeling, although I may well be wrong, that you are running away. Can that be true?"

"As it happens, it is," Iona replied. "But I have no wish to talk about it, my Lord."

She smiled at him.

"I will be very happy, if it suits you for me to stay or rather hide for a while in your house. I will be delighted to pay for the accommodation by cooking for you, as you may say, with a professional touch."

"That is the best contract I have ever been offered," the Earl answered jovially.

He held out his hand and Iona put her hand in his.

As his fingers closed over hers, she had the strange feeling that she was taking a step into the unknown without having the slightest idea of where it might lead her.

THE BARBARA CARTLAND
PINK COLLECTION

Titles in this series

THE BRIDE RUNS AWAY

BARBARA CARTLAND

Barbaracartland.com Ltd

THE BARBARA CARTLAND PINK COLLECTION

Dame Barbara Cartland is still regarded as the most prolific bestselling author in the history of the world.

In her lifetime she was frequently in the Guinness Book of Records for writing more books than any other living author.

Her most amazing literary feat was to double her output from 10 books a year to over 20 books a year when she was 77 to meet the huge demand.

She went on writing continuously at this rate for 20 years and wrote her very last book at the age of 97, thus completing an incredible 400 books between the ages of 77 and 97.

Her publishers finally could not keep up with this phenomenal output, so at her death in 2000 she left behind an amazing 160 unpublished manuscripts, something that no other author has ever achieved.

Barbara's son, Ian McCorquodale, together with his daughter Iona, felt that it was their sacred duty to publish all these titles for Barbara's millions of admirers all over the world who so love her wonderful romances.

So in 2004 they started publishing the 160 brand new Barbara Cartlands as *The Barbara Cartland Pink Collection*, as Barbara's favourite colour was always pink – and yet more pink!

The Barbara Cartland Pink Collection is published monthly exclusively by Barbaracartland.com and the books are numbered in sequence from 1 to 160.

Enjoy receiving a brand new Barbara Cartland book each month by taking out an annual subscription to the Pink Collection, or purchase the books individually.

The Pink Collection is available from the Barbara Cartland website www.barbaracartland.com via mail order and through all good bookshops.

In addition Ian and Iona are proud to announce that The Barbara Cartland Pink Collection is now available in ebook format as from Valentine's Day 2011.

For more information, please contact us at:

Barbaracartland.com Ltd.
Camfield Place
Hatfield
Hertfordshire AL9 6JE
United Kingdom

Telephone: +44 (0)1707 642629
Fax: +44 (0)1707 663041
Email: info@barbaracartland.com

THE LATE DAME BARBARA CARTLAND

Barbara Cartland who sadly died in May 2000 at the age of nearly 99 was the world's most famous romantic novelist who wrote 723 books in her lifetime with worldwide sales of over 1 billion copies and her books were translated into 36 different languages.

As well as romantic novels, she wrote historical biographies, 6 autobiographies, theatrical plays, books of advice on life, love, vitamins and cookery. She also found time to be a political speaker and television and radio personality.

She wrote her first book at the age of 21 and this was called *Jigsaw*. It became an immediate bestseller and sold 100,000 copies in hardback and was translated into 6 different languages. She wrote continuously throughout her life, writing bestsellers for an astonishing 76 years. Her books have always been immensely popular in the United States, where in 1976 her current books were at numbers 1 & 2 in the B. Dalton bestsellers list, a feat never achieved before or since by any author.

Barbara Cartland became a legend in her own lifetime and will be best remembered for her wonderful romantic novels, so loved by her millions of readers throughout the world.

Her books will always be treasured for their moral message, her pure and innocent heroines, her good looking and dashing heroes and above all her belief that the power of love is more important than anything else in everyone's life.

"Have you noticed when you are in love that somehow the air is cleaner, the sky is brighter, the colours of flowers are sharper, music goes straight to your soul, food tastes delicious whatever you eat and the one you love is so different from anyone else in the whole wide world? And they say that love is 'a many splendoured thing'!"

Barbara Cartland

CHAPTER ONE
1895

Iona Langdale woke up slowly and, seeing the early morning sun creeping in through the sides of her curtains, thought that if today was fine then tomorrow would be too.

Tomorrow was very important to her, as it was to be her wedding day.

The fuss and commotion over arranging everything had kept everyone in the house busy for nearly a month.

Now she knew that if she looked out of the window she would see the huge marquee erected on the lawn where her guests would be received.

Below, sloping down to the lake, were the barrels of beer that were to be drunk by the workers on the estate and those who lived in the village.

There were to be fireworks at night and Iona knew that everyone locally would be present at what to them was a very special occasion.

When her father had died over a year ago, she had been pressed by every member of the family to get married as soon as possible.

"You cannot possibly live in this vast house all by yourself," they said. "While we have arranged a rota to come here to look after you, we cannot do it for ever."

They had laughed before they added,

"Our husbands would strongly object for one thing, although you have offered them excellent shooting in the winter and your marvellous horses to ride, they still prefer being at home and having everything their own way!"

Iona had laughed at this, but she knew it to be true.

Her aunt and cousins had found it rather a burden to be always chaperoning her when they had their own lives and families to attend to.

Nevertheless, they had all been very kind, but she knew if she was honest that they would all heave a sigh of relief tomorrow when she came down the aisle on the arm of her husband.

It had almost seemed like Fate taking a hand when Sir John Moreton, who was the only son of the late Lord Lieutenant, had asked her to be his wife.

For a start their estates almost touched each other so that they would be able to join them together as one.

So Sir John would have Iona's estate as well as his own to manage and she had thought that he was looking forward to it.

It would be a change to have him running the estate and looking after her rather than her aunts and cousins who always complained that they had had to give up so much of their own interests when they arrived to stay with her.

'I am very very lucky,' Iona thought, as she gazed out of the window and imagined what a commotion there would be tomorrow.

Yet it was an event that the local people would talk about for the rest of the year.

Naturally she was to be married in the same Church where she had been Christened.

The local Vicar owed his stipend to her and he was engaged to perform the Wedding Service and Iona felt that everything had been arranged as it ought to be.

Her own household was providing the food that everyone would surely enjoy.

'I am sure this is the perfect way to be married,' she thought now to herself, 'with everyone round me who has known me since I was a child and who were fond of Papa.'

Her father had certainly been very generous where the village was concerned and she knew that their estate pensioners boasted all over the County that they received more generous pensions than anyone else.

It was understandable, because Lord Langdale was an exceedingly wealthy man.

He had not only inherited the huge estate and house when he came into the Barony, but his wife, Iona's mother, was a great heiress.

Both her money and her father's were inherited by their only child.

Iona was fully aware that her father had always hoped that he would have a son, but sadly her mother was not very strong.

While she lived until she was over sixty, it was not possible for her to have another baby after Iona was born.

Iona often thought it was unfair for her to have so much, especially the magnificent horses that her father had bought and bred, which he was exceedingly proud of.

'Of course,' she had said to herself, 'I ought to have a brother who could ride them faster and better than I can and who would be thrilled, as my father was, every time he won a race at Newmarket.'

She had been well aware that, because she was such a very rich heiress, her relations were always worried that she would be married for her money rather than for herself and would therefore be unhappy.

They warned her not once but many times against fortune-hunters.

When she 'came out' in London and became the '*Debutante* of the Year', they would scrutinise, she could not help noticing, every man who danced with her and she became tired of being warned against fortune-hunters.

Also she was exasperated by the fact that whenever she had asked a new man to stay, her aunts examined him, as if through a microscope, to find out if he was a genuine gentleman or, as they put it, 'someone after her money.'

When she told the family that she had promised to marry Sir John Moreton, they had been delighted.

The Moretons were an old family in the County and John's father had been an extremely good Lord Lieutenant. Everyone respected him and when he died John had taken his place in their affections.

As Iona had known John ever since she was a child, it would make things easy for him to step into her father's shoes and run the estate with the same expertise as he did.

She had always been fond of him and he was five years older than herself.

She admired the way he rode, the way he shot and the fact that he was very popular amongst the villagers.

Because she had looked on those who lived in the village almost as if they were related to her, she thought that the men from London, who considered themselves of great stature, would look down on the villagers.

They would perhaps treat them as if they were of no particular consequence and not as her father had done as if they were his children to be looked after and protected.

The house that she lived in – Langdale Hall – was mentioned in the Doomsday Book and had grown more and more majestic throughout the centuries.

The Picture Gallery was so full there was hardly room for any more and the library was bursting with books.

'It's my home and I love it so much,' Iona reflected as she stood at the window.

4

It was marvellous to think that she would not have to go away and leave it because she had a husband and she was sure that she and John would be very happy together.

He had always been kind and considerate to her and even when she was very small he had taken care of her when they were out hunting.

'He loves me,' she pondered as she stood at the window, 'and, as I love him too, we will be very content.'

She then asked herself what she was going to do for the last day of her freedom.

She knew before she even asked the question that she would walk round the garden and in her own way say goodbye to her childhood.

'When I am married with a husband to look after me as well as our children, we will be as happy here at The Hall as I have ever been,' she told herself.

As she could now see the men coming up the drive who she knew would be working on the final arrangements for the wedding, she dressed herself quickly.

For today, the last day of being alone, she did not want to talk to anyone and she merely wanted to think of her future with her husband.

She had to admit during the last year that there had been moments of great loneliness.

Of course she had enjoyed having her relations to stay, but it was not the same as her beloved parents.

'John would understand how touchy a family could be if one was favoured more than the other,' she thought. 'And John will prevent any members of the family from being jealous of me because I have so much money.'

She gave a deep sigh as she thought of how much she had given them in presents and she had paid for their education as her father had done and made sure that those who desired a ball could afford to have it.

They were grateful. Of course they were grateful.

At the same time she was quite sensitive enough to realise that they resented her being so rich when they were the same age as she was and she was a *woman*.

If she had been a man, they would have accepted her gifts far more eagerly and appreciatively.

She had never expressed such feelings aloud and now John would be ostensibly the giver of money, horses, parties, education and everything else the family looked for and hoped that they would receive.

'I am happy. I am very happy,' Iona thought as she ran downstairs and unlocked the front door.

It was still not yet six o'clock when the servants would come on duty and the dew was thick on the grass as she went to the end of the lawn where the shrubbery began.

She had always loved the shrubbery as a child and in it was her Wendy house where she kept her dolls and many other playthings.

It was where she often sat alone and planned what she would do when she was grown up.

What she wanted more than anything else was to travel, but it had not been easy to leave her father, who was, in his last few years, too ill to travel himself and he wanted her beside him almost every hour of the day.

When he had first suffered with his heart and the doctors had said that he had to live a very quiet and simple life, it had put an end to Iona's hopes that they would visit countries all over the world.

And, when this proved impossible, she had stayed with him and contented herself with reading once again of all the marvellous places she hoped to visit one day.

Now, she thought, it would be best to travel before they started a family.

She and John would be able to visit the Pyramids which she had always longed to see. They would go to Constantinople and the Greek Islands before they reached India and the Himalayas.

'There are so many places I want to go to,' she thought, 'and with John nothing could be more exciting or more thrilling.'

When she reached the Wendy house, she could see all the dolls that had always lived there.

She then walked round the little house touching her dolls and feeling, in what she thought was quite an absurd way, that they should come to her wedding.

'I want everyone and everything I have ever loved to be there in the Church tomorrow,' she told herself.

Because she was happy, she walked down the little cascade that ran from the top of the shrubbery then through the orchard.

She remembered the way she had looked eagerly for the first plums and had searched in the walled garden for the first strawberries.

'I may well have been an only child,' she mused to herself, 'but everything here is part of me and my life. I will always love it, even when I am too old to be excited as every child is by the first strawberries of the Season, the first cherries and succulent grapes from the greenhouses.'

She was laughing inwardly at herself for being so sentimental as she walked through the orchard feeling the early morning sunshine warm on her face.

It seemed to make everything around her glitter as the sun was shining so brightly.

At the end of the orchard there was a field through which ran a small stream and beyond it was a wood.

It was the wood where Iona, as a child, had really believed that there were goblins working underground and fairies flitting amongst the wild flowers.

In the very middle of the wood there was a secret pool where the mermaids lived.

One of the first things she had done every morning, when she had taken her favourite horse, was to ride to the wood and see the squirrels climbing up the trees and the rabbits running through the undergrowth.

It was a wood that she felt had played a big part in her life.

She could remember her Nanny telling her to look for special mushrooms where the fairies had danced the night before and had told her stories while they ate their tea in the little wooden hut by the pool.

'It will always be full of memories for me,' Iona thought, as she walked along the mossy path. 'One day I will bring my children here and tell them the same stories that Nanny told me.'

It was then, as she came to the centre of the wood, she saw a horse tied up, cropping the grass by the pool.

She knew, with a leap of her heart, that John was there.

He must have come to the wood, because it was in the little wooden hut that he had asked her to marry him.

It therefore made it sacred in her mind.

'John has felt he must see the place that mattered so much to him too when he was young,' she felt. 'Perhaps, as I am doing, he is thinking how wonderful the future will be for both of us.'

As there was no sign of him, she knew that he must be inside the wooden hut.

'He will be surprised to find me here,' she thought, as she walked eagerly towards the hut.

Then, as she drew near, she was astonished to hear the sound of voices.

John was not alone and Iona wondered who was with him.

Because she thought it would be a mistake just to walk in, she went to the back of the hut.

She could hear John's voice and then to her surprise it was a woman's voice who replied to him.

Iona went nearer still.

As she reached the back of the hut and stopped near the window which was in bad repair with two of the panes of glass broken and others cracked, she heard John saying in his deep attractive voice,

"You must not be unhappy, my dearest one. There is nothing I can do about it. It is just Fate."

"I prayed and prayed," the woman with him said in a whisper, "that you would somehow – find the money that you need."

Iona drew in her breath.

She now knew who John was talking to.

It was Mary, the Vicar's daughter whom she had known ever since she was a baby and who was one year older than herself.

"I prayed too," John added. "But Fate is against us and, as I am very fond of Iona, I will try to make her happy."

"Of course you will," Mary replied. "At the same time I will love you – as I always have. I always hoped, as you did, that one day we could be – together."

Her voice broke on the last word and Iona knew that she was crying.

"My precious, my darling," John said. "It's no use. We have looked at every possibility. I have no idea how my father kept on for so long when he was so hard-up."

There was a distinct pause before he continued,

"But the house is falling into disrepair and there is no money to spend on it. If the horses have to go too, what would I have to offer you?"

"The only thing I ever wanted," Mary sobbed, "and that is – your heart."

"You have it, you know you have it. I have loved you since you were a small child," John answered, "and you know I could never love anyone else the same. But how could I possibly ask you to slave for me in a house which is falling down on our heads. If we had children, we could not afford to have them properly educated."

He spoke almost harshly.

"But we would be together," Mary said. "Oh, John, why did you not get that job you told me your friend was offering that you thought would one day make you rich?"

She spoke hesitatingly because she was still crying.

As her words were muffled, Iona reckoned that she was crying against John's shoulder.

"I am afraid that my friend had raised my hopes unnecessarily," John replied with a sharp note in his voice. "He offered me what sounded a very promising position, but I had to put five thousand pounds into the project."

"Five thousand pounds!" Mary exclaimed. "Oh, John – is that what he wanted?"

"He said, if I went in on equal terms with him, I must contribute towards it," John said miserably.

He gave a laugh that had no humour in it.

"I could not have given him the money in pennies let alone in gold!"

"No, of course not," Mary said. "It was unkind of him to raise your hopes."

"He thought that he was doing me a favour. I could hardly explain to him that I was poverty-stricken."

There was silence before John went on,

"That was why, my darling, when I had no hope of ever being anything but poor, I proposed to Iona and she accepted me. I want you to understand that I have never stopped loving you. It's just completely impossible for us to be together."

Mary gave a sob.

"I understand, I do – understand," she said. "But it has been an agony beyond words to know I have lost you."

"You will never lose me completely," John replied. "I will always love you. Once I am married to Iona, I will make certain that your father's stipend is doubled and that you have everything you have ever wanted."

"I don't want anything but you," Mary wept. "I love you. I love you and I don't know how I can bear life in the future without you."

"I feel the same," John answered. "But, as Iona has been generous enough to accept me, I will do my best to make her happy and run the estate for her."

"Which you will do brilliantly," Mary murmured. "It was not your fault, but your father's, that your land has gone to rack and ruin."

"Papa was very ill the last year of his life. I don't think he had the slightest idea that things were as bad as they are. It was only after he died and I went through the accounts that I realised it myself."

John sighed before he went on,

"He loved his horses and so could not resist buying a new one from time to time, which he could ill afford."

"Everyone admired and respected him," Mary said, "but no one knew that he was so poor."

"I did not know either," John told her. "He put his money into various 'get-rich-quick' schemes that of course failed and although he kept trying he was always unlucky."

"Now it's incredibly unlucky for you and for me."

"I know, my own darling, but you have to be brave about this. There is nothing else I can do, *nothing*!"

There was a poignant silence for a moment.

"If I could have obtained five thousand pounds for the house and land," John then continued, "I might have invested it with my friend until the money poured in and then we could have been married."

He spoke as if he was just telling himself a story and then, as Mary gave another sob, he added,

"We just have to be brave. I promise that you will benefit from my marriage in every way possible."

"We have loved – each other," Mary replied, "for five or is it six years and – I just cannot imagine my life without you, John."

"I feel the same, Mary, I always believed that one day Fate would be kind to us and we would be able to marry, but now that is completely impossible. I can only promise that you and your father will be comfortable and not have to worry where the next penny is coming from."

"But I want you! *You!*" Mary sobbed. "Once you are married to Iona it would be best for us not to see each other again – alone."

"Do you really think I could bear that?" John asked. "Of course I will see you and talk to you. I swear on all I hold Holy that I will never love anyone as I love you."

"I can say the same," Mary whispered. "But what good is it when we know we cannot be together – ?"

"You have to be brave. I can only hope that one day things will seem better than they do at this moment."

Iona listening, knew that he was now kissing Mary, kissing her wildly, passionately and despairingly.

Because she was afraid that they might come out and see her, she moved quickly back down the mossy path.

Running as fast as she could through the orchard and into the shrubbery, she reached the Wendy house.

She opened the door and, breathless from the way she had rushed away from the hut, she threw herself down on the sofa.

Could it really be true what she had just heard?

Having heard it all she knew that it was impossible now for her to marry John.

She had never thought for a moment that he loved anyone else and she must have been very blind not to have guessed in the past that he had been seeing Mary, but no one had apparently ever connected their names together.

'What can I do?' she asked. 'What can I do?'

She could *not* marry John tomorrow.

It was impossible to tell him that she had overheard him and Mary declare their love for each other.

'I cannot marry him,' Iona told herself. 'Yet, if I don't, I will leave him to starve.'

It seemed at that moment as if the whole world was tumbling around her shoulders.

It was almost as if the house itself fell in on her and crushed her beneath it.

Yet what she had heard must be the truth.

It was like a huge fence that was too high to jump.

There seemed no way out of the predicament she found herself in as she sat with her eyes tightly closed.

She felt everything that she had ever known had fallen to pieces at her feet and she had no idea how to put them together or what she must now do.

Sitting there in the Wendy house, she could see, as she had out of her window, the huge marquee filled with her guests from London and the County.

She could see all the villagers, having cheered her at the Church, hurrying to the barrels of beer and food.

The children were already excited at the idea of the fireworks that would be let off after she and John had left for their honeymoon.

As the last thought sped through her mind, Iona put her hands up to her face.

What sort of a honeymoon would it be when all the time he would be thinking of Mary sobbing bitterly?

Mary would sit white-faced but silent while she and John proclaimed their marriage vows in the Church.

'I cannot do it,' Iona told herself. 'How could I do it and sacrifice him, Mary and myself?'

Because she was so desperate she clasped her hands together and prayed,

'Please God show me a way out of this, there must be something I can do. But I cannot marry John.'

Then, almost as if it was a message from Heaven, an idea came into her mind.

An idea that was so outrageous that she could not believe she was really thinking it.

Yet undoubtedly it was the answer to her prayer, an answer that would solve her problem at least for a time.

CHAPTER TWO

Iona then slipped through the garden gate and to her relief she saw that there was not yet anyone about.

She ran upstairs to her bedroom and, letting herself in, she locked the door in case one of the housemaids had seen her and wondered if she wanted anything.

She crossed over the room as the sun was streaming in through the windows.

It was shining on the inkstand on her writing desk, which was French ormolu and Iona had always been very proud of it when writing letters to her friends.

She sat down now and wrote a letter to her elderly aunt who was more or less the Head of the Family.

"Dearest Aunt Matilda,

I have just received a letter to say that my dear old Governess, Sarah Dawson, is dying and particularly wants to see me before she does.

I feel that I must go to her, as she was so kind and sweet to me when I first started my lessons.

I know it will cause problems to put off the wedding. At the same time I cannot refuse to go to Sarah when she has asked me so fervently to do so.

Please make my apologies to everyone so they will not be too upset.

Love, Iona."

She read the letter through, put it in an envelope and addressed it to her aunt.

Then she hesitated for a moment over the next letter which was to be to John.

After some hesitation she finally wrote,

"*My dear John,*

Please forgive me, but I have decided unfortunately very late that I do not wish to be married at the moment.

It would most certainly be a disaster if I changed my mind once the ring was on my finger.

I need time to think things over and I am going away to my old Governess, who has asked for me on her deathbed.

Please persuade the family not to try to find me or to prevent me from staying with her until she actually does pass into the next world.

As I know, you have spent a great deal of money and time on arranging our wedding and I am sure that you will be sensible and not offended if I give you back the money you must have expended and this will give you a chance to put your estate back into good order.

As you will see from the cheque, I have not put to whom the money is to go to, so you can write in any name you want and I suggest we keep it a secret.

Forgive me, forgive me for upsetting you but I must have time to consider marriage which is such an important step into the unknown.

As you know, I am very fond of you, so I cannot help feeling that we are doing everything too hastily and so therefore I am running away.

Again please forgive me.

Love, Iona.

She then took her chequebook out of a drawer and wrote out her cheque for five thousand pounds, which she was sure John would send to the man who had offered him a Partnership.

The next cheque she made out was for ten thousand pounds.

She knew that neither of them would matter to her life in any way at all, but they would certainly make a huge difference to John's.

She placed the two cheques in an envelope with his letter and addressed it to him and left it beside the one to her aunt on the writing table.

Then she jumped up and went into the room next to hers where there were three wardrobes filled with dresses and clothes.

What she was looking for, pushed behind one of the wardrobes, were some suitcases that she always used when she was going away for a short visit.

They would hold all the dresses she would need for at least several weeks.

As she took the simplest and least flamboyant ones from the wardrobes, she thought it would be a mistake to look too smart or to attract attention in any way.

As she had always done things very quickly in her life, she managed to fill the two cases in very quick time.

Then she went to her bedroom to collect her brush and comb and her face cream.

When everything was in the cases, she closed them and went to the door and opened it softly to see if anyone was about.

The floor outside was dark and silent.

But she thought she heard a movement from below stairs as if the housemaids were brushing the carpets in the sitting rooms and passages.

Carrying her cases and she found them quite heavy, she crept along the passage, having closed her door and put on it a note saying boldly, *do not disturb*.

It would prevent her lady's maid from calling her or bringing up her breakfast.

There was a narrow staircase that was only used by the servants, which ascended at the end of the corridor. It led to the room that was occupied by her secretary.

Mr. Masterton had been there in her father's time and he was now growing old, but he was most efficient in paying the wages for the estate and in the house.

Iona was certain that he would have drawn out a good deal of money to pay the extra people who would be engaged for her wedding day.

As she opened the door, the room was in darkness.

Then, as she pulled the curtains back, she could see how neatly Mr. Masterton had everything arranged.

Fortunately she knew where he kept the keys of the safe where there was always plenty of cash.

When she unlocked the safe, she found that she was not mistaken. In fact, at a quick glance, she decided that there was at least one thousand pounds there, if not more.

She had purposely taken her biggest handbag with her and she transferred the money in notes into it.

Then she filled another bag with coins that she put into one of her cases.

She left a note on the safe to tell Mr. Masterton what she had taken and signed it.

She quickly pulled the curtains across the window and hurried into the passage that led to a garden door at the side of the house. It was bolted to keep out burglars, but she pulled them back and stepped out into the sunshine.

Shutting the door behind her, she put her suitcases by it and then she ran as quickly as she could to the stables.

She did not go to where the horses were kept, but instead she went to the building at the far end of the stables where the carriages were housed.

Here was kept the present her father had given her when she was a child when he had first taught her to drive – a donkey cart.

It was, she thought at the time, the most exciting gift she had ever received.

Because there had been a small pony to pull it, as her father had said, in less than a year she had learnt to drive as well as he did.

He had then given her a slightly bigger carriage that could be pulled by two ponies, which were a sheer delight to Iona as they were faster and she enjoyed driving them as much as she loved riding her father's hunters.

She felt that the donkey cart would be unobtrusive and if she travelled alone people would not be surprised. Whereas if she drove a chaise, they would obviously think it strange that she had no groom with her.

With some difficulty she found the boy who was on duty at night, who had fallen asleep on the hay in a stall.

She sent Ben, for that was his name, to fetch her cases.

"I have to take them to someone in the village," she said, as she knew he would remember it if he was asked.

But he was thinking, as she wanted him to, that she was giving a present of clothes to someone she favoured.

It took Ben only a short time to fetch two ponies and fit them into the shafts of the donkey cart.

They were part of a team and there were two other ponies which matched them perfectly and were capable of drawing the smart chaise her father often travelled in.

For a woman to be driving a team unaccompanied was, Iona knew, to attract attention and that was the one thing she wished to avoid.

When the two ponies were placed in position in the donkey cart, she picked up the reins, thanked Ben, and then drove off.

She noticed that he was yawning and felt that he would not be in a hurry to tell the rest of the staff where she had gone.

As they would all be talking about the wedding, it was unlikely that they would ask him if anything unusual had happened.

She had risen so early that morning that it was not yet seven o'clock as she drove out of the yard, her head held high.

Avoiding the main drive, she took a route through the fields that led to the very end of the village.

Iona thought with some satisfaction that she had got away without anyone seeing her.

When it was realised that she had disappeared there was only Ben who had seen her go and, as he was rather a stupid boy, it would be a long time before anyone found out that she was actually missing.

The problem she had now was where she could go.

If she stayed in the County, she would have, if she was discovered, all her family begging her to come back.

And what was more, they would plead with her to change her mind and marry John.

She therefore decided that, as her Governess, whose deathbed she was supposedly going to, lived in the North, it would be in the North that they would expect to find her.

What they did not know, and she had not told them, was that Sarah Dawson had died nearly a month ago.

She had sent flowers to the funeral, but had been in London at the time, so those in the country had not even been told of her demise.

It was doubtful if the servants would remember her as she had only been a Governess to Iona when she was ten and two years later she had gone to a school in London.

There had been so much chatter about her wedding that it had never occurred to her to tell the old servants who would remember Miss Dawson that she was now no longer in this world.

'It was clever of me to think of her,' Iona reflected as she drove on. 'I know that dear Miss Dawson would have been glad to help me.'

Even as she thought of this, she wondered just how many of the staff who were employed now would want to help her do anything quite so outrageous as to cancel her wedding the day before it took place.

She could imagine all too clearly just how angry her relatives would be, thinking it extremely wrong of her to cause such a commotion at the eleventh hour.

She was very certain, however, that not one of them would imagine for a single moment that she was running away from marrying John.

They all thought him charming and handsome and were more relieved than they dared put into words that he was taking her off their hands.

They had most certainly done their best, Iona had to admit, in keeping her well chaperoned whether she was in London or the country.

Although it might at times have been very tiresome for them, they had all benefitted from the money and the many presents she had given them.

At least, she thought, she would not have to send back all the presents she had received, as at the moment they would merely think that the wedding was postponed.

It was only as time passed, and if John was tactful, they would accept that it was never actually going to take place.

As she drove on and the sun became brighter and hotter, she wondered again where she should go and where it would be possible for her to hide.

In her anxiety to disappear as quickly as she could, it had not struck her that she might find it difficult as a young girl alone to stay in comfortable hotels.

But she could not think of anyone with whom she could hide from her family.

There were several cousins who lived in Sussex and Kent, but she was determined to avoid those Counties.

She knew only too well that if any of her relatives, however distant, came in contact with her, they would then merely notify her aunt.

She, being her nearest relative would be absolutely furious at the way that Iona had disappeared without even telling them where she was going.

They would undoubtedly think it quite mad of her to trouble herself so much over an old Governess, rather than be the bride at what was a very smart Social occasion.

'I am sorry that I will upset them so much,' Iona said to herself.

At the same time she asked,

'How could I marry John when he loves Mary and she loves him?'

For the first time since she had eavesdropped their conversation she could not help thinking that they had, in fact, treated her somewhat shabbily.

Then she thought that one could not help love.

It was either there or it was not.

Although she had loved John in her own way and had been willing to marry him because he was so kind and helpful, she realised that if she was honest she did not love him in the same way that Mary did.

He was so handsome, so charming and so pleasant to be with.

But the way Mary had spoken of her love for him and he had replied with his, told her, if she was truthful, that her love was not as great as theirs.

'I do love him,' she thought, as she drove on, 'but I suppose in a way it is the same as I loved Papa and would have loved my brother, if I had had one.'

She stopped and then her thoughts continued,

'I felt that John protected me and is one of the most charming men I have ever known. But there is surely more to love than I was receiving from him or giving.'

She was working it out for herself while the ponies, clearly delighted to be given their heads, were increasing their distance from Langdale Hall.

'I will go to the sea,' Iona decided, 'and I am sure that no one will think of looking for me there.'

The difficulty was she was not certain where they would look for her.

Because she had gone alone, without a groom and without a lady's maid, they would, she was sure, think that she would be staying with friends and doubtless search her address book for their names.

'I have to be very clever and make sure that I am not carried back after only a few days of freedom,' she told herself.

She could imagine only too clearly all the fuss they would make over her disappearance and how they would try with every means possible to force her to marry John, despite the fact that she had run away from their wedding.

'I can honestly say that I don't love him as much as I thought I did,' Iona told herself.

But she knew that her family would not listen.

'If John has any sense,' she mused, 'he will pay his friend the five thousand pounds he was asking for and stay with him until our marriage is completely forgotten.'

How they would talk. They would talk, talk, talk, coming to the conclusion that poor John was to be pitied.

Two hours must have gone by before she realised that having had no breakfast she was rather hungry.

As she was keeping away from the main roads and travelling down narrow lanes, it took her some time to find a small Posting inn.

It looked quite respectable and, when she drove the ponies into the stable yard beside it, there appeared to be no sign of any other carriage.

When the ostler then took charge of the ponies and promised to provide them with plenty to eat and drink, she went into the inn.

It was a small building with low ceilings, but clean and the aged publican bowed to her politely.

"Is there anythin' I can do for you, miss?" he asked.

"I had to come away from home in a hurry," Iona replied, "and would therefore be grateful if I could have something to eat and coffee to drink."

The publican smiled.

"That'll not be difficult, miss. If you'll come this way, I'll take you into the dinin' room."

It was a dark room with long windows overlooking a garden at the back of the inn.

It did not take long before she was served with eggs and bacon, which were well cooked, and coffee that was drinkable if not particularly tasty.

She found out from the publican exactly where she was and it was still quite a long way from the sea where she wanted to be eventually.

She was amused, however, to find that the publican was surprised that she was travelling alone and rather than tell him she inferred that where she was going there would be people much older to look after her.

"You must be ever so careful of yourself, miss," he said. "If it's not them 'ighwaymen, then there be plenty of slippery fingers to take anythin' of any value from you and them be very fine ponies you be a-drivin'."

"I will be very upset if anyone steals them."

"Then you must take extra care, miss," he repeated. "I've 'eard tales about someone like yourself who's woken up in the mornin' in a hotel to find that 'is good 'orses 'ave been replaced with them as wouldn't fetch a threepenny bit at a sale and there be no way of 'im gettin' them back."

"I will be very careful with my ponies," Iona said, "because I love them very much and, as you can see, they are very well bred."

"That's why I be a-warnin' you if your father and mother let you drive around alone without a friend or a servant beside you."

He spoke in a fatherly way that rather charmed her.

At the same time she felt a little streak of fear just in case her ponies were taken away from her.

Then she told herself that it was the way one would expect a man, living in the depths of the country, to think about the world outside.

She paid him for her breakfast and for the food the ostler had given the ponies.

As she took his hand to say goodbye, he said,

"Now you take good care of yourself, miss. You be a very pretty young lady and there be 'ighwaymen who'd be more interested in you than your 'orses."

Iona laughed.

"I promise you I will take the greatest care of both and thank you for looking after me so well."

He helped her into her cart and waved as she left.

She waved back, thinking that at least he was very friendly and now that she was all alone in the world she needed friends wherever she could find them.

She travelled on, stopping later in the day at a not so pleasant inn for a quick luncheon.

Then she set off once more, still hoping it would not be long before she reached the sea.

However, she realised at about six o'clock in the afternoon, when the sun was not so strong and was now beginning to sink in the sky, that her ponies were tiring.

They had kept up their pace all through the day and she knew that she was a long distance from home.

Tonight, at any rate, they would not be looking for her and she need not be afraid of staying anywhere where a 'nosey parker' would think it strange that she was alone and would be able to inform the family about her.

It was, however, difficult to find a nice Posting inn like the first one she had first stopped at.

When finally she found an inn, she was not the only guest staying there.

There were a number of common-looking men who were travelling together and one elderly couple.

And there was one man by himself who Iona, when she entered the dining room, realised was looking at her in a way she disliked.

She deliberately sat in a seat where she had her back to him.

But, when she was just finishing the rather dull and heavy pudding she had been served, he came to her table and sat down in the seat opposite her.

"If you're travelling alone," he said, "and I'm doing the same, it seems to me we should introduce ourselves."

As Iona thought that it would be a mistake to be rude, she replied,

"If you want to talk then I am afraid that you will be disappointed. I am very tired after travelling a long way today and am going straight to bed."

"You cannot be so unkind as to do that," he said. "I've had a damned awful day too. The fella who I was supposed to meet didn't turn up and another who's usually more friendly said he was too busy to waste time on me."

"It does sound very hard," Iona murmured.

"What you're saying is that nothing would interest you, but I'd like to know where you are going."

"I am going to the sea," Iona told him, "but it is taking longer than I expected and those who are waiting for me will wonder why I have not arrived earlier."

"Well then, their loss is my gain," the man replied. "Now come on, you be friendly and I'll stand you a drink. What would you like? Whisky or red wine?"

"You are very kind," Iona answered, "but I would like nothing because I never drink anything alcoholic. As you can see, I am having lemonade, which unfortunately I am certain has never encountered a fresh lemon!"

The man laughed.

"That is true enough. Now please let me get you something to cheer you up. What about a cherry brandy or something with a bit more kick in it."

"Thank you, but no," Iona replied, "but I am very tied and so I am going up to bed. Perhaps we will meet at breakfast, although I am leaving very early."

"I've a better idea than that," he smirked.

Iona had risen as he spoke and now he rose too and, when she walked towards the door, he came beside her.

There were people talking in the hall and, as she went up the stairs and he accompanied her, she thought it a mistake to stop and say goodnight to him while the other people were listening.

She reached her bedroom, which was on the first floor and it was, she thought when she had first seen it, a rather shabby room and not particularly clean.

She stopped at the door and held out her hand.

"It is nice to have met you," she said. "But, as I have told you, I am leaving early tomorrow morning."

"Allow me to unlock the door for you," he offered, taking the key from her hand.

She let him do so, but as the door opened, to her horror he walked into the room.

For a moment she just stood in the open doorway looking at him.

Then he said,

"Now come along. You are alone and I'm alone. I'll make sure that you're not lonely if nothing else."

For the first time Iona was aware of the danger she was in.

Swiftly, before the man realised what she was about to do, she turned and ran down the stairs.

She burst into the room she had seen the publican of the inn come from when she had arrived.

He was sitting at his desk at the far end of the room and she ran towards him saying breathlessly,

"There's a man in my bedroom and I don't know how to get rid of him."

The publican rose slowly to his feet.

"A man in your room!" he exclaimed. "But is it someone who's stayin' in the inn?"

"Yes, he was in the dining room," Iona said, "and he followed me upstairs and I am very tired and want to be alone. But he has pushed his way in and I am afraid, very afraid."

The publican looked at her as if questioning if she was being truthful.

Then he said,

"Go to the next room where you'll find my Missus and I'll see what I can do about this man who's upsettin' you."

"Thank you, thank you!" Iona replied. "I am sorry to be a nuisance, but, as I am alone, I don't know how to make him behave himself."

"You go and talk to the Missus and I'll see what I can do," the publican suggested.

He walked out and Iona opened the door at the far end of the room.

It was obviously the publican's sitting room and his wife was there holding a baby in her arms.

The woman looked up as Iona entered.

"If you be wantin' anythin'," she said, "but I can't come now. I've got me son to put to bed."

"Your husband said – I could sit with you," Iona replied, "while he deals – with a man who is being very tiresome."

"Oh, not one of them! We gets them all the time 'ere. But you leave it to Bill, 'e'll cope with anyone. So sit down till 'e comes back."

She pointed to a chair near the fireplace and Iona sat down feeling suddenly very tired and very frightened.

The woman was rocking the baby gently in her arms.

"Is that your son?" Iona asked.

"It's one of them," the woman answered. "I 'as three sons and two daughters and they be an 'andful I can tell you that."

"They must be if you look after them yourself," Iona said sympathetically.

"Two of them be quite a bit older than the rest and they be 'elpin' me with the little uns but then it's Bill who suffers. He's short-'anded and it's difficult to get reliable people to work for one these days."

"I think it's very brave of you to have a hotel and such a large family," Iona said.

"That be true," the woman answered, "we be at it night and day and there'll be visitors who arrive long after we've gone to sleep. Then Bill 'as to pull on 'is clothes and find them a room. It ain't all sugar and spice I can tell you, miss."

"I am sure it's not," Iona said. "I did not think this sort of thing would happen because I was travelling alone."

"Bill tells me you were a pretty young girl and 'e 'oped there wouldn't be no trouble. It's usually the girls who stir things up round 'ere especially when the men 'as had more to drink than be good for them."

Iona felt herself shiver.

Then, as the baby started crying, there was nothing she could do but wait for Bill's return.

It was nearly an hour before he came back and both his wife and Iona looked at him questioningly as he came into the room.

"Another of them," he said to his wife. "This one'd talk the 'ind leg off a donkey!"

"What did he want?" his wife enquired.

"Need you ask," her husband replied. "This young lady's too pretty to be travellin' alone and she's bound to 'ave trouble wherever she goes."

"Now you are scaring me," Iona said. "Have you sent him away from my room?"

"I persuaded 'im to join others who was playin' bridge, but it weren't easy, I'll tell you that. It cost me a large glass of whisky that I 'opes you'll be payin' me for."

"I will certainly do that," Iona replied, "and thank you very very much for saving me."

"Oh, Bill can do anything if 'e wants to," his wife said. "Anyone who comes 'ere and causes us trouble, 'e won't 'ave 'em again and who can blame 'im?"

"Who indeed," Iona sighed, "and thank you more than I can say."

"Now you takes 'er upstairs and show 'er 'ow to lock 'er door," Bill's wife said. "When that man finishes 'is whisky, 'e'll no doubt 'ave another try, you mark my words!"

"I thought he might do that," he added. "I've tested the lock and there be nothin' wrong with it. If she locks 'erself in and 'e 'ammers on the door and I 'ears him, I'll go out and give 'im somethin' to get on with."

"Well, 'urry up about it," his wife said impatiently. "I want to go to bed and you were up late last night, so you must be dead tired."

"I certainly am," Bill agreed. "So come on, Missy, up the stairs. I'll show you 'ow to lock the door so that no one can get at you, unless they crawl underneath it and your friend be too fat in the tummy for that!"

Iona smiled at him.

"Thank you! Thank you for being so kind. I never thought that this would happen to me."

"That's good advice, you can take it from me," his wife pointed out. "It's pretty young women like yourself who causes all this trouble. Now come along, it's time my poor 'usband 'ad a bit of shut-eye."

"I will go up the stairs at once if you will be kind enough to escort me," Iona replied.

"Come on then," Bill said, "and unless 'e breaks the door down 'e won't be able to get at you. That I promise!"

Iona said good night to his wife and then hurried up the stairs with Bill beside her.

The room was empty, but he had left the candles on the dressing table.

"Here be the key," Bill said. "Turn it in the lock when I've left you and don't open it however much 'e begs you to do so."

"No, of course not. I would not think of doing anything like that."

"Well, you take my best advice," Bill insisted, "and don't go stayin' in this sort of place. It's all travellin' men can afford and a pretty girl like yourself be fair game."

He glanced round the room as he spoke almost as if he expected to see someone under the bed.

Then, putting the key in the lock, he said,

"Turn it as soon as I'm on the other side. Then pull up one of the chairs and put it against the door in case 'e tries to force it open."

"Thank you! Thank you! I am so grateful."

Bill left and Iona did as he had told her and put a very heavy chair against the door,

"Goodnight," she shouted after she had done so.

"I'll see you in the mornin'," Bill answered and she heard him go down the stairs.

She then pushed the door with both hands to make sure that it was closed and was convinced that it would be difficult for even a strong man to force it open.

Then, because she was afraid, she only took off her dress and stockings, leaving the rest of her underclothes on as she climbed into bed.

At first she listened, afraid that the man might come back and try to find her, but, because she was actually very tired, she fell asleep very quickly.

*

When she awoke, it was morning.

She looked at the clock and it was half-past seven.

She must have indeed slept peacefully through the long hours after Bill had shown her how to lock herself in.

There had been no more trouble and now her one idea was to leave the inn as soon as she could.

'I must never, never,' she scolded herself, 'stay in a place like this again.'

At the same time she was thinking that it might be very difficult to find anything better on her odyssey.

CHAPTER THREE

Driving with not too much speed down the narrow lanes, she was wondering what was happening at The Hall.

She reckoned that they would have found her letters when she did not go in to change for dinner yesterday.

She could imagine all too clearly the horror of her relatives and it would have been quite impossible for them to stop the guests travelling from London for the wedding.

As friends were staying in the house, it meant they would continue to exclaim at the extraordinary behaviour of Iona and the trouble it had meant when everything had to be stopped at the last minute.

First of all Iona thought, as she drove on, that they would have to notify the Vicar.

Then the men who were organising the fireworks would have to be told as well as the caterers.

Apart from all that she wondered what John would say to her family, if, as she expected, they had seen that she had written a letter to him as well as to her aunt.

He was bound to turn up if only to verify the fact that she really had disappeared and, extraordinary though it seemed, no one knew where she had gone.

One or two of her older relatives would remember Miss Dawson, but the rest would not have set eyes on her.

It was easy to imagine, however, the consternation of the whole house.

The small bridesmaids she had chosen from among her relatives would perhaps be the most disappointed.

Doubtless the wedding cake would be put on one side and kept for what everyone imagined would be Iona's return home once her old Governess had died.

She could not help thinking, however, that the one person who would be delighted would be John.

She was certain that he would be tactful enough not to mention the fact that she had given him any money, also saying that the wedding was postponed and not cancelled completely, as she had made clear to him in her letter.

The people from London would return disappointed and there would not be a hue and cry for her which Iona was afraid might happen if they really believed she had run away completely from the idea of marrying John.

She felt that she had caused everyone a great deal of trouble.

Equally she asked what else could she have done.

And how could she marry John when he was in love with Mary?

If, as he would believe, he could join his friend's Company, they would be able to be married in six months' time without everyone thinking that it was particularly odd.

She reassured herself with these thoughts.

But, because of what had happened last night, she was now thinking about herself in a very different way.

She had driven off yesterday quite certain that she could just disappear for perhaps three or four weeks.

Then she would return home to tell them firmly that her marriage to John was cancelled completely and she had no wish to marry anyone.

It would give them something to talk about and to complain about again as they had complained before that she could not live at The Hall without being so heavily chaperoned.

She had thought that it would be easy to stay away until all the trouble had blown over.

What had happened with that man last night had really terrified her.

So she was now wondering how, because she was alone, she would manage to stay somewhere quiet and safe for at least three or four weeks.

She supposed it had been very stupid of her not to anticipate that a young girl alone driving expensive ponies would obviously cause comment.

And the fact that she was young and pretty would attract men as she had attracted that horror last night.

'What can I do? Where can I go?' she asked again.

Thinking it over she thought maybe she would have been wiser if she had let one of the older members of the family into the secret that she had discovered about John and Mary.

And she could have asked her to take care of her until she could return to The Hall.

But, when she thought it over, she had few elderly relatives who were unmarried or who had members of their family living with them.

She did not trust any of her female relations not to gossip about what had happened and, of course, they would whisper the story secretly. It would be passed on from mouth to mouth until they all knew the truth.

The truth, if nothing else, would be most unfair on John.

Iona was determined that she would not hurt him even if she was humiliated by the fact that he was marrying her for her money and not, as she had believed, because he really and truly loved her.

'Perhaps no one will ever love me,' she reflected sadly.

Naturally men would cluster round her as they had done in London and, as an heiress, there would always be fortune-hunters pursuing her and perhaps she would not be clever enough to recognise them.

At the same time it was not only her money but the magnificence of The Hall that shone behind her just like a huge jewel that was the envy of everyone who saw it.

It all came back to one question, she thought,

'What shall I do?'

She drove on through the day, wanting to get away from that inn and the man who had tried to enter her room.

Then she realised, although she had bought some food in a small village and the ponies had been watered but not fed, that she had to find somewhere before it was dark.

It was just before five o'clock when she drove into a rather pretty little village.

It had thatched roofs on the cottages and brightly painted gates that opened into small flower-filled gardens.

'I wonder if there is a Posting inn here?' she mused.

But there only seemed to be rows of cottages and a rather larger building that she thought must be a school.

Then she saw a shop ahead and she thought perhaps that there was someone who could tell her if there was a Posting inn close to this village.

She pulled up outside the shop.

As there were two boys playing on the pavement, she asked them to hold the ponies while she went inside and they were eager to do so.

They ran to the ponies' heads and patted them and talked to them in a way that told her that they were used to horses and not afraid of them.

Carrying her handbag, she walked into the shop and it was a typical small village shop.

It held everything from soap and socks to, at one end of it, fresh bread and sausages.

There was an elderly man with a kind face behind the counter.

He smiled and greeted her,

"Good afternoon, ma'am, what can I do for you?"

"I have just driven into the village," Iona replied, "which I think is very pretty. I wonder if you would be kind enough to tell me if there is a hotel here or a Posting inn where I can stay the night with my ponies?"

"Now that be a difficult question," he replied to her. "The nearest place for visitors like you, ma'am, be some miles away and I've heard complaints about the food."

Iona gave a little sigh.

"There must be somewhere. I have been driving all day and my ponies are now tired and hungry."

The man scratched his head.

"I be thinkin'," he said, "where a young lady like you could go. It be difficult to find anywhere round here."

"Oh, please try to think of somewhere – "

She was about to ask if there was perhaps someone private who would put her up for the night if she paid.

Then before she could say the words, the shop door opened and an elderly woman came storming in.

Moving quickly she almost pushed Iona to one side as she walked up to the counter.

"I'm not stayin' another minute," she said, speaking loudly. "I've 'ad enough! As I've said before, 'enough is enough' and I'll take *no* more of it!"

She seemed to almost scream the last words and the man behind the counter asked,

"What's happened, Mrs. Jones?"

"Need you ask!" she shouted. "He's failed again in what 'e be seekin' and I swear 'is temper shook the roof!"

She gave a deep sigh before she went on,

"It shook me a lot when 'e comes into the kitchen to complain about the tea and then vents his rage on me because he can't find what 'e wants. No one, you mark my words, no one will ever find that – "

"Now sit down, Mrs. Jones," the shopkeeper said. "Let my wife bring you a nice cup of tea."

"I'm not stoppin' for tea or for anythin' else," Mrs. Jones replied. "I've come to tell you what's 'appened, because it'll be *you* who'll 'ave to find someone else."

She shook her fist before she continued,

"I'm not sittin' there to be sworn at by any man, let alone 'is Lordship. I'm sick to death of 'is tantrums and that's the right word for them."

As she said the last words, she walked out of the shop slamming the door behind her so violently that Iona was surprised that the glass in it did not break.

She then turned to the shopkeeper and asked,

"What has happened? What has upset her?"

"You may well ask," the man answered rubbing his forehead. "This has happened afore and it'll happen again. But it's me, always me, who has to bear the brunt of it, to find his Lordship someone else to do the cookin'."

"Why is he so disagreeable?" Iona asked.

The shopkeeper gave a short laugh.

"You may well ask. There's many people who've asked that question. It's one that everyone who lives here knows the answer to. There's no mistake about that."

"Then naturally I am curious," Iona said. "I have never seen anyone so upset."

She looked round the door almost as if she expected the woman to be outside, but she had obviously gone.

Iona wondered if she was telling other people in the village the reason why she was so upset.

Almost as if he knew what she was thinking, the shopkeeper said,

"It be very sad, very sad for his Lordship and sad too for us."

"What is sad?" Iona asked curiously.

"Well, if you don't know and you stays here long enough, everyone'll soon tell you. It be a tragedy and no mistake. It seems to me there be no way of preventin' us all from sufferin' as his Lordship be sufferin'."

"Who is his Lordship?" Iona asked, feeling perhaps that she might have heard of him.

"He be the Earl of Woodbridge. And, although he loses his temper, he has every reason to do so."

He spoke in a way that made Iona very curious and then she said,

"Do tell me why. It all seems very strange to me."

"It seems very strange to us too and we has to put up with it."

"Put up with what?" Iona questioned impatiently.

She was now even more intrigued and it seemed odd that the shopkeeper should speak in this way.

The fury of the woman who had given in her notice was different from anything she had ever seen before.

"Well, his Lordship's uncle was strange enough in his ways," the shopkeeper said, "and I suppose it upset him a great deal when he inherited the title to find the money he should have had was hidden and could not be found."

Iona was now completely fascinated.

"What do you mean it was hidden and could not be found?" she asked.

"What I said, miss. The old gentleman was very old, nearly ninety when he died and he were a miser. He never spent a penny if he could help it."

The shopkeeper shook his head.

"His fortune, that I hears was quite a big one, was hidden by him so that no one could steal it. I can assure you it was somethin' none of us in the village would have done anyway, even though he were such a miser."

Iona was finding this compelling. It was the sort of mystery she always enjoyed.

Sitting down in a chair by the counter, she begged,

"Please tell me more. It sounds like a Fairytale and I can hardly believe it's true."

"It be true enough to us, miss, because we suffered from him. We all thought it'd be different when the young Lord took his place."

"Surely he is not a miser too?" Iona asked.

"No, because he has nothin' to hide. When he goes to look at what his uncle had left him, he finds it had all been hidden somewhere in the house or in the grounds or even in the lake and no one has set eyes on a penny of it."

Iona stared at him.

"I don't understand," she said. "If he had money, even though he was afraid it might be stolen, why should he hide it anywhere but in a bank or a safe?"

"That be just what we has asked ourselves, miss. We thinks, as his Lordship did when he arrived, that all he had to do was to look around the house, put the key in the lock and Hey Presto there it'd be."

The way the shopkeeper spoke made Iona laugh.

"But it was not there?" she quizzed.

"Not a sign of it. It were then he began to lose his temper. He cross-examined everyone in the village who be old enough to talk. 'Someone must have some idea where the money is,' he said, not once but ten thousand times."

"I don't believe it. It's the most fantastic story I have ever heard. Do you really mean that the old Lord has hidden the fortune?"

"A very big fortune from what I hears of it, miss. Thousands and thousands of pounds, he just kept a bit of it to feed himself and to pay the wages of them who served him. Very mean he were too, givin' them hardly enough to keep body and soul together."

"So he was a real miser," Iona said. "I call that fascinating. I have never met one and have often wondered why they become misers in the first place."

"If you ask me it's because they hate others to such an extent they wants it all for themselves. I can remember his old Lordship scowlin' at me when I takes him a bill. He'd scrutinise it as if he expected I'd deceived him and then grumbled as he always thought it were too much."

"What makes you think he had a fortune to hide?"

"Well, for one thing it was in the newspapers when his father died that the Earls of Woodbridge were rich and his Lordship's mother had been an heiress.

"The money cannot have disappeared!" Iona cried.

"But it has, miss. We knows for sure before the old gentleman died that he were hidin' away any extra pounds or shillings he had at the end of a week."

"You mean he hid it in the house and the grounds?"

"Sometimes they'd see him diggin' away at night or in the early mornin' before anyone went to work and when they tells the new Lord what they had seen, he digs up the place quick enough, but finds nothin'."

"You mean someone had stolen it?"

"No, he found a better hidin' place, you can be sure of that, but I've no idea where it could be."

"It's just the most riveting story I have ever heard," Iona said. "Do you really think that there are thousands of pounds hidden in the house or in the grounds?"

"When the old Earl first came here, he were a real nice chap with a kind word for everyone. He helped those who were ill or who needed help. Then we knows that he visits the bank in town and they tells him the money's been paid to his Lordship every week and then it disappeared."

"You mean every week he hid it somewhere?"

"We knows he did that as he draws out of the bank more than he needs and then he puts the rest in some secret place that no one can find."

"I can hardly believe it!" Iona exclaimed. "So how long has the new Lord been looking for the money?"

"For over three years and it's changed him from what seemed to us all when we first saw him, a nice young man, into a creature who frightens everyone who works for him and has them runnin' away in a fury like Mrs. Jones."

"She was certainly upset," Iona said, "and one can understand it. Equally I feel very sorry for the poor man who cannot find the hidden treasure."

She was thinking as she spoke that lack of money did strange things to people.

In fact it had made John ready to marry her even though he loved Mary with all his heart.

There was silence and then the shopkeeper gave a deep sigh.

"I expects in the mornin' his Lordship'll want me to find him a new cook and I doubt if anyone else in the village will go up to Woodbridge Court. They've all left sayin' they'll stand no more of it and the way Mrs. Jones was speakin' of what had happened will be no help."

Iona drew in her breath.

Then she asked in a very quiet voice,

"Was Mrs. Jones the cook?"

"She were and a good cook she be too. She's won many a prize in the village when they has a competition as to who makes the best cakes. I've always heard that her soups be delicious too."

Iona was silent for a moment and then she said,

"I can see that you are in rather a fix and have no one to take Mrs. Jones's place. I am considered a good cook and I would be very glad to stay at the house and it would give my ponies a good rest too."

The shopkeeper stared at her.

"Well, if that ain't Manna from Heaven, I'll eat my hat. Do you really mean it, miss, that you could cook a proper dinner for his Lordship. Three courses I believe he has and he pays for the best food, I'll say that for him."

"I am sure I can satisfy his Lordship for tonight if not for longer," Iona said. "As I have already told you, my horses must have a rest before they go much further."

The shopkeeper flung up his hands.

"It's a miracle, it really is!" he exclaimed. "I was just thinkin' I would have to send the Missus up to get his Lordship's dinner and her says the last time her went it'd be the last and she wouldn't go again even if the Queen herself were askin' her to do so."

"Is it as bad as that?" Iona quizzed him.

"I don't want to put you off," he went on, "but he has a bad temper when he don't find what he's seekin' and they all hide when they hears him comin' back from where he were diggin' empty-handed."

"Well, if I only stay for a night," Iona said, "you will understand. But I promise you that the dinner will be excellent as long as I have the right ingredients."

"I knows his Lordship's likes and dislikes only too well," the shopkeeper said. "If you'd help me over findin' him someone now Mrs. Jones's walked out, I'll thank you from the very bottom of my heart and that be the truth."

"I will be delighted to help you," Iona replied, "and if I only stay a day or so at least you will have time to look round for someone else."

"It'll not be easy, miss. His Lordship's tantrums be known all over this part of the County and he must have had twenty cooks by now."

"As I will be number twenty-one, perhaps I will be able to stay until you find someone who will be number twenty-two without any difficulties," Iona smiled.

"You're the kindest lady I've ever met. Now I'll take you up myself to show you the kitchen and we'll take with us what food I think his Lordship will require."

"If he is not stingy about the food, that is at least something in his favour," Iona commented.

The shopkeeper laughed.

"He be only too glad to have a great deal more than he has, but the reason for his temper be that he's run out of his own money and it's not much from all that I've heard."

Iona was quiet for a moment and then she said,

"I am rather vague about these things, but surely, if there was such a large fortune, then there must be money coming either to him or to the bank every month."

"Now that be a good question to ask, miss, and one that most people would not be intelligent enough to ask."

"What is the answer?" Iona enquired.

"You'll hardly believe this, but the old Earl draws out all he has in the bank and borrows a great deal as well."

The shopkeeper shook his head.

"He tells them that he's improvin' the estate which were completely untrue and they lends him the money," he continued, "which means that now he's dead they're payin' back themselves from what does come in and the new Earl therefore has to live on what he can sell. That's one thing that makes him angrier than anything else."

"Oh, now I understand," Iona said. "He is selling treasures from the house."

"One goes every month or so, just to keep his head above water, as they be heirlooms handed down through the centuries, his Lordship minds very much partin' with them. I can't help thinkin' that's the real reason for his temper."

"I cannot blame him for that. It must be infuriating when he knows that the money is somewhere in the house or on the estate, but he cannot find it."

"He's certainly tried and no one can say he ain't. But so far he's not turned up one penny piece."

"Yet he is quite certain it is really here?"

The shopkeeper nodded.

"Yes, he's very sure. He's had a full account from the bank of the money they lends his uncle and the money they pays him, but not sight nor sound of it anywhere."

Iona was even more intrigued and it really was the most extraordinary story she had ever heard.

She could not help feeling sorry for the new Earl and whatever she had to do, it would be exciting to stay there for the night.

It was certainly not the sort of place where any of her family were likely to look for her.

It was then that the shopkeeper came from behind his counter and started to put sausages and bread from the far end of the shop into a large basket.

As he realised that she was watching him, he said,

"His Lordship won't be at all pleased with the bill for these. But he'll not see it until you've fed him tonight and perhaps tomorrow – "

He paused a little before he said the last word and looked at Iona enquiringly.

She grinned.

"To please you I will stay as long as I can. As I have already said, I want my horses to have a good rest."

"You'll give me one, too," the shopkeeper smiled. "I has a headache every time I thinks of findin' someone else for his Lordship, but then they had their pride and they won't put up with his temper."

As he finished speaking, he took off his apron and put on his coat.

"You be my best customer who's ever walked into this shop today or any day," he said. "I be more grateful to you than I can say."

He laughed as he went on,

"I only hopes you'll last long enough for me to get my breath back, so to speak. It's what I loses when the cook at The Court says 'goodbye' and in the same way as Mrs. Jones expressed her desire to leave."

"I will try not to be so noisy or so positive about it. Actually it's a challenge to see if I can succeed where they have failed," Iona replied.

"I'll be prayin' you do," the shopkeeper said.

He opened the door as he spoke.

Then as if he suddenly remembered he shut it again and ran across the shop and through another door which opened in the opposite direction.

He left it ajar and Iona heard him shouting,

"Ma! Ma!"

There was silence and she looked round the shop.

Then she said to herself,

'This is certainly an adventure I did not expect. At least it means that we will be safe tonight.'

She was certain of one thing.

If the Earl was intent on finding his hidden treasure, he would not be pursuing her in the same way as the man at the inn had pursued her last night.

She gave a little shudder as she remembered how frightened she had been.

She told herself that in a gentleman's house, strange though he might be and with a reportedly bad temper, she was not likely to attract his attention unless he was cursing her for producing a badly cooked meal which he had found intolerable in Mrs. Jones and his other cooks.

When she thought of the delicious food she had had at The Hall because her father had always employed the very best chefs possible, she could not help smiling at the idea of doing the cooking for a man who was notorious for his bad temper and in a house that she had never seen or heard of before.

But at least it meant safety for tonight and, unless she was mistaken, good accommodation for her horses.

Next the shopkeeper came back through the door into the shop.

"I'm ready now," he said, "and I'll take you up to the Big House so that I can show you the kitchen before his Lordship finds out that Mrs. Jones has left."

He paused to smile at her.

"When he does," he continued, "he'll tell me to find him someone else and I don't mind sayin' it'll be really hard as the village has had enough of him now to last them a lifetime."

"I can see it's very difficult for you," Iona replied.

By this time they had walked outside and the boys were still holding the ponies as she had told them to do.

She gave them each a two shilling piece and they stared at it with delight.

Then the shopkeeper said sharply,

"Come along boys! What do you say to the lady? I'm sure you've got manners as your mother always taught you to have."

"Thank you! Thank you!" the boys chorused.

Then, as Iona climbed into the driving seat and the shopkeeper sat down beside her, the boys said cheekily,

"'Urry up and get back 'ere, Mr. Hopkins, 'cos we wants to buy some of your sweets."

"I'll not be long," the shopkeeper replied.

As he spoke, Iona started off the ponies and they sped down the road she had driven down earlier.

As she had seen no grand gates before she reached the shop, she was certain that they must be further ahead and she was not mistaken.

They had only driven a little way before the gates came into sight and were as impressive as she had expected them to be with two lodges.

As she saw the long drive with oak trees on either side, she felt that she had been luckier than she expected.

At least tonight she would be in a building that was not unlike her own home.

'This is such an adventure,' she told herself. 'A real adventure and, in bringing me here, God has been kind and tonight, at any rate, I will not need Bill to protect me.'

They travelled on a little further down the drive and there was a stately bridge crossing what appeared to be a lake with a stream running into it.

Then there was a large courtyard in front of what Iona realised was a magnificent house.

It must have been built originally in the reign of Queen Anne and Iona thought that it was a perfect example of the good taste which was prevalent in that reign.

The front door and the steps up to it had a carved stone lion on either side.

She only had a quick glance at the house before the shopkeeper indicated with his hand that there was a large entrance on one side that Iona guessed led to the stables.

She drove the horses up to it and then, as she drew them to a standstill, an elderly groom came out through the stable doors.

"Evenin', Mr. Hopkins," he said. "I didn't expect to see you 'ere."

"I've brought you a new cook," he replied.

The groom threw up his hands.

"I'd 'eard there'd been trouble, 'as 'er gorn?"

"Yes, she be gone, but I've brought you another, although she might not stay any longer."

The groom chuckled.

"That be too much to ask. But if it keeps 'is Nibs 'appy for tonight we can sleep in peace."

"I hope so," Mr. Hopkins replied. "Her horses need food and drink just as you do."

"They'll not go 'ungry, I promise you that."

The groom turned towards Iona.

"It be nice to see you, miss," he told her. "I only 'opes you be comfortable 'ere."

"Thank you," Iona replied. "I am very grateful to Mr. Hopkins for bringing me here."

"'E'll bring you with pleasure," the groom laughed, "but it be takin' you away that makes 'im cry. Ain't that true, Jim?"

"Now don't you be puttin' ideas into her head," Mr. Hopkins said. "I hopes this young lady'll stay and she tells me she be a good cook."

"That be just what 'is Lordship needs and I'll see these fine 'orses be as comfortable as she'll be."

Iona smiled at the groom.

"Thank you very much. I know the horses, which are very precious to me, will be safe and happy with you."

"You can be sure of that, miss," the groom said, "and I promise you the 'orses 'ere always 'as enough to eat even if their Master don't!"

Iona thought this was the first kind thing she had heard about the Earl, but she did not say so aloud.

The two men were now taking her luggage out of the dog cart and, carrying her cases, Mr. Hopkins walked across the stables to where Iona saw there was a narrow path leading, she supposed, to the kitchen quarters.

Her own house was built in much the same way and she thought that it would not be too difficult to find her way around.

They walked in through a side door and down long passages, passing larders and sculleries before they came to the kitchen.

It was exactly like the one she had at her home with a huge beam over the top from which hung dead birds and animals and a large number of onions.

There were two big stoves just as they had at home and, although there were some pots and pans on the table, it appeared as if Mrs. Jones had indeed left in a hurry.

However, the room was clean and the fire in the stove was still burning and Mr. Hopkins was looking round as if to make sure that everything was correct and present.

Then he said,

"I suppose I should have told you that there's no help in the kitchen as his Lordship cannot afford to pay anyone."

Iona thought for a moment and then replied,

"I tell you what I will do. If you send me someone just to help with the washing-up and anything else that I may need, I will pay her myself. I have a little money with me."

Mr. Hopkins looked at her in surprise.

"Are you sure you can afford it?" he asked.

"Quite sure. I have been lucky lately and, as I love cooking and hate the washing-up, I will be very glad if you could send someone from the village to help me tomorrow, if not tonight."

"All right," Mr. Hopkins agreed. "I'll do what you ask me, but don't go spendin' all your money here in case you has to leave in a hurry."

Iona smiled at him.

"I hope I will not be thrown out nor have to leave in the same rage as Mrs. Jones did. You have been so very kind in letting me stop the night somewhere where I know I will be safe and where my horses will be looked after."

She felt a shiver go through her.

"I was very scared," she went on, "that there would not be a place I could stay except perhaps miles away."

"Well, you'll be safe here at any rate. If there be any trouble you come back to me. I shouldn't go lookin' for his Lordship. Just put the food on the table."

Iona did not speak for a moment and then she said,

"I did not think to ask, but surely there are other servants in this large house, even though he has quarrelled with the cook."

"I should have told you," Mr. Hopkins answered, "but I didn't think of it."

There was a short pause before he carried on,

"Yes, there are a couple, a man and his wife, who live here."

Iona looked at him in surprise.

She was thinking of the large number of servants she had at The Hall and even then they often complained that they were overworked.

He was obviously thinking over his words.

"I'd be dishonest if I said more were not wanted," he replied. "But, as his Lordship cannot pay them, not unless he sells some more of his treasures and he's eking out what he's got on the sale of the last one, he won't employ any more."

He sighed before he added,

"I suppose he'll soon have to sell a bit of the silver what's been in the family for years."

"I can understand," Iona said, "that is what he has no wish to do."

She knew how much she would mind if she had to sell any of the treasures at The Hall and felt very sorry for the Earl.

"Well, you do the best you can," Mr. Hopkins said in a brisk manner, as if he was afraid to talk any further on what was obviously a controversial subject.

"I promise you I will do," Iona replied. "Please do come and see me tomorrow morning and by that time I will know whether the meal I will cook his Lordship tonight is good enough or if I have to leave."

"If you asks me, his Lordship will be glad to have anythin' to eat tonight. I don't suppose he knows that Mrs. Jones has really gone, otherwise he'd be on his way to me to find him someone else."

"Well, perhaps I will surprise him," Iona said. "I will try to do so because it will help you and I am very grateful to you, Mr. Hopkins, for being so good to me."

She put out her hand as she spoke and he took it.

Then he said,

"You've got a lot of pluck for a young girl. Good luck to you and I hopes things will seem quite different in the mornin'.

He walked towards the door as he spoke and Iona smiled at him.

"Goodnight," she said, "and thank you."

"It's me to be thankin' you," Mr. Hopkins replied, "and so it's goodnight and good luck!"

With that he was gone.

Iona looked round the kitchen with a faint smile on her lips.

'Whatever else I was expecting for tonight,' she told herself, 'it was not this!'

CHAPTER FOUR

Iona looked at the basket she had brought with her from the village shop and saw that it contained what she considered quite enough to make a good dinner.

Then she poked the fire and added some more coal and wood to it before she started to look for the pans she would require to cook the food in.

All was going well and she was just wondering if she ought to find the dining room, as she supposed that it would not have been made ready for his Lordship.

Suddenly the door of the kitchen opened slowly and a man peeped in.

Because he was obviously doing it surreptitiously, she only saw the top of his head which was grey.

Then, as he saw her, he stood up and walked in with an expression of surprise on his face.

"Who are you?" he asked. "I suppose Mr. Hopkins sent you to take Mrs. Jones's place."

"You are quite right," Iona replied.

"Well, I'm the butler," the man said, "and I've been here for more than thirty-five years. My Missus, who's the housekeeper, be afraid when his Lordship loses his temper. So I takes her away and we hides till he's himself again."

Iona looked at him in astonishment.

It was surely the strangest behaviour she had ever heard of in all the years when her father had the house filled with servants.

As if the butler was surprised, he said,

"Of course we must do things properly. My name's Newman and I'd be glad to hear yours, miss."

Iona, during her drive, had already decided that on no account must she use a name that would be recognised by her family.

At the same time she wanted to be sure that she would remember it herself.

She therefore called herself 'Ida Lang' which she was sure no one would connect with her real name.

"My name," she told Newman, "is Lang, Ida Lang, and I obliged Mr. Hopkins by coming here and taking the place of your cook as I was present when Mrs. Jones told him in no uncertain terms that she had walked out."

"As they all do sooner or later," Newman replied bitterly. "I were thinkin' that unless Mr. Hopkins comes up trumps there'd be no supper for any of us tonight!"

"Well, you need not worry any more about that," Iona said. "I have brought a basket full of food and I was just beginning to plan a meal for his Lordship."

"And for me and the Missus too, I hopes," Newman asked hopefully. "Now me legs be playin' up I can't walk down to the village as I used to and his Lordship usually sends the groom with a list of his requirements."

He gave a laugh as he added,

"Usually that's when we've nothin' and no one, not even his Lordship when he's in a temper, wants to starve."

While Newman was talking, Iona was placing on the table everything she needed to cook the meal.

She thought of using only a little from the basket, but she now realised that there were two others to be fed.

"I sees," Newman said, "that you're goin' to give his Lordship enough to fill his stomach, so I'll go to lay the table in the dining room. I'll also tell the Missus that the coast is clear and she can come out of hidin'.'"

He was gone before Iona could reply.

She thought this was certainly a place for surprises and she could hardly imagine the housekeeper at The Hall hiding from anyone, least of all her father or herself.

'I had better give his Lordship a good dinner and then perhaps he will be in a good temper,' she told herself.

Next she started filleting the bones off a large fish that she thought might have been caught locally.

She was standing at the stove with a frying pan in her hand when Newman came back.

Holding onto his arm was an elderly woman who Iona guessed must be his wife.

She had a kindly face and must have been pretty when she was young, but now she looked rather frail.

Her hand, when she put it out to Iona, was shaking.

"I am thankin' God," she said in a quavering voice, "that you are here, otherwise his Lordship might go hungry and then he would be even angrier than he was today."

"I don't think he will go hungry with the dinner I have prepared for him," Iona answered. "There will be plenty for the three of us, unless Mr. Hopkins does find us someone, as I have asked, to help with the washing-up."

She paused before she added,

"I love cooking, but I hate the mess it makes."

She laughed and then she saw that Newman was looking at her with a worried expression on his face.

"I don't want to frighten you away," he said, "but Mr. Hopkins has as much chance of findin' someone to come here and do the washin'-up as flyin' in the sky."

Iona stared at him.

"Is it as bad as that?" she asked. "Surely, however angry his Lordship may be, it need not affect those he pays to work for him."

"That be just the point, miss. His Lordship don't pay anyone. Those who've come and helped clean up the place out of kindness or rather respect for the house itself have gone away empty-handed."

"You mean he does not pay any wages?" she asked.

Newman shook his head.

"He just ain't got the money. It be as easy as that. He's sold almost everythin' he brought here when he came and, as you must have heard, in big houses everythin' of value be entailed onto the next owner when this one dies."

Iona gave a little cry.

"Of course it does, how stupid of me. I did not think of it. Mr. Hopkins did say things were very difficult and the Earl is desperate as he is so in need of money."

She stopped for a moment before she added,

"I did not think of anyone living in a house as large and as impressive as this as being completely penniless."

"Well, that's the truth, miss, and there be no way of makin' it better not unless his Lordship finds the treasure his uncle's hidden, which we've all searched for without findin' a sign of it."

"It's the most extraordinary story I ever heard. Are you quite certain the treasure was buried in the house?"

"We thinks it must be," Newman replied, "because his Lordship has searched everywhere outside."

He sighed again before he continued,

"His late Lordship, before he died, wrote in his will that, when the treasure was found at last, there were certain people he admitted owing money to and two others who he wished to benefit by what he had left behind him."

"So he said that in his will?" Iona asked.

"Yes, it were written soon after he comes here. All I can tell you is that I sees him year after year, getting' more mean about partin' with as much as a single penny and ever more secretive as to where he put his money."

"But you know that he actually did hide it here in the house?" Iona queried.

"He hides it all right, miss, but, when he was doin' so, we were told to go into the kitchen and stay there. It were not worth riskin' our jobs to be a peepin' Tom."

"I can understand that!" Iona exclaimed. "But you must have some idea of where it was hidden."

Newman made a helpless gesture with his hands.

"This house be as big as any Army Barracks. The estate be the largest in the County so how are we to know."

Iona laughed because it sounded so ridiculous.

And she knew by the expression on Newman's face and the way his wife was trembling that they had all been terrified of upsetting his late Lordship.

"But you personally," Iona said softly, "must have some idea where he would hide the money. After all, if there was so much of it, it would not be so easy to hide."

"It weren't all gold sovereigns. There were notes as well and I suggested to his present Lordship that they might be under the carpets."

"Of course they might," Iona remarked.

"But he then turns the carpets up in every room and there were not a sign of anythin'."

"It does seem a difficult problem, but I am going to think of all the places I would hide treasure if I had it. Then you can suggest it to his Lordship or look yourself."

"All I wants is to be paid a little bit for the work we does for him," Mrs. Newman said in a frail voice. "Me husband and I are always alone. People from the village pop in and out and that be the right word for it."

Her husband laughed.

"It is indeed! They comes in and when they finds there ain't no pay and he rages at them because the treasure be still hidden, they goes away and vows never to come back again. So there be only us and us!"

He put out his hand as he spoke and placed it on his wife's shoulder.

"My wife knows I'm tellin' the truth when I says we haven't had a penny to call our own for six months."

"I don't believe it!" Iona exclaimed.

Equally she knew it was the truth and that Newman and his wife were not lying to her.

Then impulsively, as she was so sorry for them, she suggested,

"Let's for the moment talk business. I went to Mr. Hopkins' shop to ask where I could stay for the night in a quiet respectable Posting inn where they would welcome my ponies and I would have a comfortable bedroom."

She was just about to add where she would not be chased by a common man as happened last night, but then thought it wise to say nothing about it.

Instead she went on,

"I have been reckoning that if I had a good dinner, a nice bedroom and my horses were looked after and fed, it would cost me at least five pounds."

She hesitated for a moment before she said,

"So that is what I will give you now, because you are kind enough to welcome me here and, as I have already told you, I was hoping that Mr. Hopkins would send me someone I could pay to do the washing-up."

She opened her handbag, took out five sovereigns and pushed them across the table to Newman.

He stared at them in astonishment and then said,

"Do you really mean what you be sayin', miss?"

"Of course I mean it," Iona replied. "I would feel very dishonest if I did not pay for staying here in what I hope will be reasonable comfort."

Newman drew the money towards him slowly as if he could hardly believe that the coins were real.

Then he said,

"I swear to you, Miss Lang, that the Missus and me will make you as comfortable as it's possible to be in one of the best State rooms."

Iona smiled.

"It certainly sounds most luxurious and thank you both for being so kind to me. Now you had best go and tell his Lordship that dinner will be ready in an hour."

Newman looked up at the big kitchen clock.

"I've to go and put on my uniform, so the Missus'll lay the table and perhaps, miss, you'll give her a hand."

"I will. I want to see the dining room anyway."

Mrs. Newman opened the door and Iona followed her along a narrow passage past a huge pantry and then through a door covered in thick green baize.

Now she was in the grand part of the house and she realised at once that it was full of extremely fine furniture and the pictures on the walls were magnificent.

She only had a brief look at the hall and the wide passage beyond it, before Mrs. Newman opened a door.

Iona followed her into the dining room and it was even more impressive than she had expected.

There was an exceptionally fine fireplace of white marble and any owner would be proud to eat here.

The walls were panelled in what she thought was Elizabethan style and there were pictures that she thought must be of the Earl's ancestors. They had obviously been painted during their lifetime by an artist whose work today would be of great value.

In the centre of the room was a large polished table on which Mrs. Newman placed four gold candlesticks.

On the table there was a superb gold bowl in which there was fresh fruit that she thought must have come from the garden earlier in the day.

Mrs. Newman arranged the knives and forks at the head of the table.

It was all fascinating and Iona wanted to examine the pictures more closely as well as the mantelpiece which she was sure was at least three hundred years old.

Then she saw that the clock on the mantelpiece was at one minute to eight and felt that it would be a mistake if the Earl came in and found her and Mrs. Newman there.

"I will go and get the first course ready," Iona said.

She hurried back to the kitchen with Mrs. Newman following her.

By the time she had dished up the fish and the hot plate that went with it, Newman had arrived with a tray.

Iona then started working on the second course.

No one questioned whether she was a good cook, but she herself knew that she was exceptional in that she had learnt to cook from one of the most brilliant chefs her father had ever employed.

He was a Frenchman who had come to England out of curiosity and her father persuaded him to spend a month or two at The Hall.

She had been twelve at the time and, because she was a very bright and intelligent young girl, the chef had elected to teach her to cook.

As she found cooking so fascinating, he made his most unusual dishes for her and showed her how she could make them herself.

She used to learn a new dish every day to surprise her father with at dinner and, when they had friends, she would help the chef and his two scullions.

The dishes were, she remembered, at that time, the talk of all their County friends and people used to beg to be invited to the house to try the Master chef's special dishes.

When the meal was over, her father would then call her and the chef into the dining room to receive the many compliments they so rightly deserved.

Because she had been taught properly, Iona loved cooking and yet she seldom had the chance to show off her culinary talent.

She found that the English cooks they had at The Hall resented any interference at all in the kitchen and they would be furious if they thought the dish she had made was more applauded than the one they had produced.

So she had not cooked for a long time, but she had not forgotten all the skills the French chef had taught her.

Although she was short of spices, she still managed to make not only her dish of fish outstanding but also the two courses that followed it.

She felt that when she had finished that her French teacher would have been immensely proud of her.

She was just putting what was left of each dish on the kitchen table when Newman came in to say,

"His Lordship wants to thank you for the excellent meal you cooked for him, miss, and to apologise for being so disagreeable to you after luncheon."

The way he spoke made Iona realise without being told, that the Earl was not aware that his cook had left.

"Does he really want to see me?" she asked.

"He does, miss, and I thinks that you deserve every word of praise he has to give you," Newman replied. "At the same time I didn't tell him that Mrs. Jones had left."

Iona laughed.

"Save my dinner for me," she said, "in case I am thrown out as a usurper!"

"I don't thinks that's likely, but just to make sure we won't go with you. I want a taste of that fish and the next dish before it happens!"

Newman was, of course, only joking.

Iona took off her apron and pushed her hair back from her forehead.

Holding her head high, she walked from the kitchen and along the passage towards the dining room.

She told herself that she was not afraid of anyone least of all a man she had just cooked an excellent dinner for.

Even so, as he was so extraordinary and apparently terrified everyone, she only hoped she would not be thrown out of the house at least until she had spent a night in one of the State bedrooms.

So she opened the door into the dining room with some trepidation.

She saw that the Earl was sitting, as she expected, at the end of the table. He was leaning back comfortably in his high chair with a glass of port in his hand.

As she came in from the pantry door, his Lordship had his back to her.

When she had entered the room, he said,

"I would like to thank you, Mrs. Jones, for the most delicious meal I have ever had. I cannot understand why you hid your talents so cleverly that I had no idea that you could cook like that."

He sighed before he went on,

"I can only apologise for what I said to you after luncheon and I wish that you had told me sooner what a brilliant cook you are."

Iona stood inside the door while he was speaking and now she came forward.

She was aware as she stepped into the candlelight that the Earl was looking at her in great surprise.

And she too found him completely different from the man she had anticipated.

She had somehow thought of him, because of what she had been told, as being rather coarse and heavy and a man of about forty or fifty.

To her complete amazement, sitting at the top of the table there was a young man not, she thought, much older than twenty-six or twenty-seven.

And he was exceedingly handsome.

He had broad shoulders and she was quite certain that, when he stood up, he would be at least six feet tall.

Then, as she looked at him, he was still staring at her in astonishment.

Finally he blurted out,

"But you are *not* Mrs. Jones!"

"I am now taking her place, my Lord," Iona replied, "because she walked out. Mr. Hopkins, the shopkeeper, was in despair as to who he could send to take her place."

She gave a slight smile as she continued,

"So to help him I came here. Also to be honest, I wanted to find somewhere quiet to stay the night."

"And you can cook like this?" the Earl questioned. "I beg of you to not only stay one night, but as many nights as you can possibly spare."

Iona smiled.

"That is most kind of you, my Lord, but I don't want to be an encumbrance in any way."

"An encumbrance!" the Earl exclaimed, his voice rising. "Who would not go down on their knees and thank the Gods for unexpectedly finding in their house someone who could cook like the angels themselves?"

"Thank you, my Lord, but I cannot imagine that we should be hungry when we reach Heaven."

"Perhaps hunger is one of the punishments of Hell," the Earl replied. "But I am forgetting my manners."

He smiled at her before he offered,

"Please sit down and tell me why I should be so privileged by unexpectedly finding a cook in my house, who could only have learnt her skill from a French chef of the highest quality."

As the Earl half-rose to his feet, she sat down in the chair nearest to him at the table.

"You are quite right, my Lord. I learnt my talent, if that is how I should refer to it, from a famous Frenchman whose cookery books, I believe, are still selling well in this country as well as in France."

"Then I will certainly try to buy one when I go to London. I expect you have been told that the reason I cannot travel and so am imprisoned here is for the boring excuse – that of having no money to pay my way."

Iona did not speak and he went on,

"I can understand now why Mrs. Jones left me, but I am extremely surprised, in fact, astonished, at being so privileged that anyone so talented should take her place."

"As I have told you, my Lord, I wanted somewhere safe to stay for tonight and my ponies which brought me here are tired and hungry."

"I will thank them tomorrow," the Earl said, "for bringing you here. I am quite sure they are as outstanding as your food."

"I hope you will think so," Iona answered.

"Now tell me your name," the Earl demanded.

Just for a moment Iona had forgotten what name she had chosen and then after a little pause she said,

"My name is Ida Lang and, as you can imagine, I am interested in the magnificence of your house, although I have seen so little of it so far."

"But you have heard the strange unpleasant stories that emerge from it?"

He spoke bitterly and Iona felt suddenly very sorry for him.

After all, he was young, very young in fact to have inherited an ancient title and such a glorious house and estate only to find that he had no money to keep it going.

She had thought when listening to all that was said about him that perhaps, after all, he was a stupid elder son who had no idea of how to manage his house and estate.

He was still trying to find the money that must be somewhere where his uncle had hidden it.

She was thinking about him and then she was aware that he was thinking about her.

"How can it be possible," he asked, "that anyone as young and as beautiful as you, should be out alone without anyone to protect you from the dangers of the open road."

"It is because I am well aware of the dangers," Iona answered after a moment's pause. "But I was very grateful to Mr. Hopkins for taking me here."

"How did you know that the position of cook was vacant?" the Earl asked.

Iona gave a little chuckle.

"I was told all about it, my Lord, very loudly and furiously by the cook whose food you apparently did not appreciate at luncheon."

The Earl burst out laughing.

"So that," he said, "is how you managed to turn up so unexpectedly. When she told me that she was leaving, I believed her. It was only a little later when I was no longer so angry and rather ashamed of myself that I wondered if I would have to go to bed hungry."

He made a gesture with his hands and added,

"Or else have something cold and unappetising that had been left over from previous meals."

Iona laughed.

"That sounds such a sad story. But, of course, you should not have upset the poor woman in the way you did."

"It was the most fortunate thing I have ever done! Here you are and I have just enjoyed a meal more than I have ever enjoyed one before and I recognised the Parisian touch at every scintillating mouthful."

Then the Earl said in a very different tone,

"I only hope you are staying. But I will be honest and tell you, as I am sure you have been told already, that I cannot pay you for working for me."

"That I understand, my Lord. I would be glad to stay for reasons I don't wish to discuss at present, while I make up my mind where I will go next."

The Earl stared at her and then he said,

"I have the strangest feeling, although I may well be wrong, that you are running away. Can that be true?"

"As it happens, it is," Iona replied. "But I have no wish to talk about it, my Lord."

She smiled at him.

"I will be very happy, if it suits you for me to stay or rather hide for a while in your house. I will be delighted to pay for the accommodation by cooking for you, as you may say, with a professional touch."

"That is the best contract I have ever been offered," the Earl answered jovially.

He held out his hand and Iona put her hand in his.

As his fingers closed over hers, she had the strange feeling that she was taking a step into the unknown without having the slightest idea of where it might lead her.

Then, as the Earl took his hand away, he said,

"Forgive me for not suggesting it before, but will you join me in a glass of port or maybe you would prefer the champagne I had earlier with my meal, which naturally was exactly right with its French origin."

"I would love a little drop of champagne to drink your health with, my Lord, and to wish you luck."

"Perhaps that is what you have brought me. I have been in utter and total despair. Yet now, after the excellent dinner I have just enjoyed, I feel different. It must be you who is bringing me what I have been seeking."

"You mean your hidden treasure?" Iona asked. "I have, of course, heard the story from Mr. Hopkins that you are looking everywhere on your estate to find the fortune your predecessor has hidden from you."

The Earl drew in his breath and replied intensely,

"How could any man be so cruel and so insane as to hide away the very lifeblood of this house and estate?"

Iona did not answer and he went on,

"At the moment I have no money of my own and wherever I dig I find nothing – nothing at all. Yet there is supposed to be thousands and thousands of pounds hidden somewhere by my crazy uncle, who should have been put in a lunatic asylum."

"Was he frightened of thieves or people preying on him?" Iona asked curiously.

"I have no idea," the Earl replied. "Actually I only remember seeing him once or twice in my life. Although I believe my father saw him frequently in London."

"Why do you think he hid all the money in the first place?" Iona asked the Earl.

"I have asked myself that question over and over again – "

He hesitated as if feeling for words, then went on,

"It was only when his uncle died that he came into the title and, of course, an enormous fortune which should, if there had been any justice in the family, have supported him earlier."

"You seem to be a very strange family, my Lord, but then you must find, sooner or later, the fortune which is hidden somewhere in this house or in the grounds."

"It is easy to say that," the Earl retorted, "but very difficult to do more than I have done already."

His voice sharpened as he added,

"It just seems incredible that any man could have hidden so completely the large amount of money that my uncle drew from the bank on the first day of every month.

"Then he took it all away to hide it from perhaps thieves and the one person it would come to automatically on his death, which was – *me*."

He ended with such bitterness in his voice that Iona realised how furious it had made him to even think of what he was being deprived of, which was rightfully his.

But he was being, she felt, somewhat over-dramatic about it.

"Are you quite certain, my Lord," she asked, "that your uncle did not confide in anyone?"

"I have thought of that too," the Earl answered. "I have been through his diary with the greatest care. From the time he inherited to the time he died practically no one stayed in this house."

"People must have come to see him."

"They called on him because they thought it was polite, but he seldom, if ever, offered them his hospitality."

"It is exactly like a Fairy story," Iona said. "So you must believe it will eventually have a happy ending."

"How can I believe that," the Earl asked harshly, "when I have already searched high and low in this house and in the grounds for all that my uncle has hidden?"

"You cannot have dug everywhere. Quite frankly, if he was such a miser, my Lord, I don't think he would have hidden it anywhere but in the house itself."

The Earl looked at her.

"Why do you say that?" he asked almost rudely.

"I don't know," Iona murmured. "But I feel certain I am right when I say that as a miser he would have wanted to protect what he valued so highly. One does not feel that there is protection in the open air or even in the sunshine."

"I see your point!" he exclaimed. "Perhaps you are right and I have been spending a great deal of time outside when I should have been inside.

"But I can assure you that I have tapped the walls, I have looked under the floorboards and even ransacked the Chapel without finding so much as a penny piece."

"All the same, I feel sure that the money must be somewhere in the house," Iona persisted.

The Earl threw out his arms.

"Then find it! Perhaps you are lucky and perhaps you have been sent from Heaven like an angel to save me."

Iona wanted to laugh.

But he spoke so seriously that she knew it meant so much to him, so she prevented herself from doing so.

"I will try," she promised. "In the meantime I will cook your meals that will make you feel strong enough to climb to the very top of the highest tower or down into the depths of the cellar."

The Earl chuckled and replied,

"Which I am thankful to say is not empty. I was reckoning the other day that it might just last my lifetime and then it will be gone too."

"Nonsense!" Iona exclaimed. "Of course you are going to find the hidden treasure. I think I have stepped into a Fairy story and Fairy stories always end happily."

She smiled at him as she continued,

"So make up your mind, my Lord, once and for all, that the great fortune that you are looking for is here in the house and you must search until you find it."

"And you will help me?" the Earl asked.

"As much as I can, but do remember that cooking takes time and thought and I will need both of these if I am to stay here as your cook."

"Not as my cook," the Earl replied. "But as the most honoured guest who has ever crossed the threshold. You bring me the best dinner I have had for years and now fresh hope when earlier today I admit that I was almost mad with despair."

He put out his hand.

"Will you help me now that you have descended on me like an angel from the sky when I called for help?" the

Earl asked. "I have come to the conclusion that rather than fail I would rather die."

"You must not say such things," Iona said sharply. "You are young. You have to live and there are a great number of people on your estate and in the village who look to you for guidance and help."

She gestured with her hand as she went on,

"They all, I believe, pray that you will win and they are sure that they will then benefit if you do."

She felt the Earl's fingers tighten as she added,

"I will help you as best I can and sometimes I feel what the Scots call 'fey' so I just know that you will be successful."

"Now I am quite sure you are an angel," he said.

Then bending forward he kissed her hand.

CHAPTER FIVE

When Iona awoke it was very early and the sun was streaming into the bedroom through the gap at the sides of the curtains.

She was in the State room and she had fallen asleep as soon as Mrs. Newman had unpacked her cases.

She had hung her clothes in the large wardrobe at one end of the room and had also placed her hairbrush and everything she required on the dressing table.

'I have certainly fallen on my feet,' Iona thought to herself.

Then she decided to see more of the house in case she had to leave, although the Earl had said he wanted to keep her, but, as he was so unpredictable, he might easily change his mind, however well she cooked for him.

She jumped out of bed and pulled back the curtains.

'There is,' she thought, 'a great deal to be done to this room to make it clean and tidy.'

There was dust everywhere and she was quite sure that the carpet had not been brushed for months.

Equally it was a very beautiful room and she was thrilled to be in it.

She dressed quickly and, going down the stairs, was aware that no one else was about.

She let herself out of a side door, which she thought would lead to the stables and she was not mistaken.

She felt that she had been remiss in not looking at her ponies before she went to bed.

But when she left the Earl after dinner she felt sure, although she should have gone out to look, that the ponies would be all right.

She peeped into two stables before she found them and then realised that they were indeed very comfortable.

Their stalls were clean and there was fresh straw on the ground and she could see that there were buckets of water for them and food in the manger.

She patted them both and talked to them and they seemed pleased to see her.

Then, as there was no one about in the stables, she walked into the garden.

She could see the places where the Earl had been digging to find the money his uncle had hidden.

There was a large hole on one side of the carved basin of the fountain and other large gaps in the lawn.

'He surely does not expect the fortune to be hidden under the grass,' she said to herself.

Then, as she could see more places that had been dug up, she realised how frustrating it must be for the Earl to find nothing when he was looking so diligently for it.

She walked down to the lake and was surprised to find that he had cut deeply into the side of it. There were some gaping holes in the rim and bricks had been removed.

She tried to visualise how an elderly man who was a miser would store his fortune.

It seemed to her ridiculous for the Earl to think for a moment that he had buried it outside the house.

'I suppose,' she told herself, 'that he has looked all over the house from the top to the bottom before he started on the outside.'

She sensed that time was moving on and returned to the kitchen, entering by the same door she had opened earlier in the morning.

She guessed, as she did so, that it should have been locked and bolted and she was quite certain that the other doors in the house were the same.

'The old Earl must have been afraid of burglars,' she told herself, 'and, of course, people will talk not only about the furniture and pictures here. They will talk of the money that is hidden somewhere and it must be in a very clever place or the Earl would have found it before now.'

She started cooking breakfast and she was not alone for long when Newman joined her.

"Good morning," she said, as he walked in through the door that led from the pantry.

"I were just askin' myself if you be ill," Newman replied. "In fact, when I wakes up this mornin', I thinks that what happened last night was a dream!"

Iona laughed.

"I expect you will want the dream to cook you a breakfast. So sit down and let me give you your eggs and bacon right away."

Newman did as he was told.

"I says to the Missus, I says, if that pretty lady has vanished in the night I should not be in the least surprised."

"I should have been most surprised if I had had to vanish," Iona said. "I am so grateful to you for giving me such a beautiful bedroom. I slept like a top."

"I thinks you would, miss, after such a long day on the road there's not a man or woman who doesn't feel they needs a good sleep and no one to keep them awake."

Iona put the plate of eggs and bacon in front of him and then she started to make the French *croissants* that she knew would please the Earl.

She was quite relieved to find that there was plenty of butter in the larder although she had not brought it from Mr. Hopkins yesterday.

As if she had asked the question, Newman said,

"That comes from the farm. We be fortunate in not havin' to pay for it, as we haven't had to pay for all the chickens and eggs we have eaten."

Iona was thinking how at her own home everything that came from the farms was always fresh and delicious.

"I suppose there are fish in your lake? Are they edible?" she asked Newman.

"They are good enough when we can get them, but I haven't the patience to be a fisherman. The only boy who bring us one now is the boy who works in the stables, as he likes bein' with the horses but gets no pay."

"I think his Lordship is a very lucky man in having so many people working for him without payment."

"Well, I have not seen him in such a good humour as he was after his dinner," Newman said. "But then my wife has never pretended to be a cook and he's just had to have what she could manage."

"I think you have both been marvellous," Iona said, "and that is why I hope we don't take too long to find the treasure."

"Well, if anyone can find it, it has to be you, miss. As I says to the wife last night, you have been so generous to us it seems as if our luck has now changed and Manna is comin' down from Heaven when we least expected it."

Iona laughed.

"I have been called many things, but not 'Manna'."

However, she was speaking to deaf ears because at that moment both she and Newman heard the Earl's voice coming from the dining room.

"I am ready for my breakfast," he was calling out loudly.

Newman thrust a piece of bacon into his mouth and then, pulling on his coat, hurried out of the kitchen.

He left the door wide open and, as Iona dished up what she had been cooking for him, she could hear the two men talking in the distance.

She put everything on a tray and, as Newman came back, she said,

"Now it's all ready for him. He will have to wait a moment for his coffee."

"That be somethin' he has complained about every time when my wife has made it for him, but I thinks he will be all smiles this mornin'."

"I do hope so," Iona replied anxiously.

She was tidying up the table and wondering if Mr. Hopkins had found her someone for the washing-up when Newman came back.

"His Lordship's now as pleased as punch over your *croissants*," he said, "and hopes you have some new ideas for luncheon. I've never seen him in such a good mood."

"I will think of something."

As she spoke there was a knock at the kitchen door.

Newman opened it and there was an elderly woman standing outside.

"Good mornin', Mrs. Barley," he said. "And what brings you here?"

"Mr. Hopkins tells me you wants 'elp in the kitchen and I'll be paid for it. I'm not comin' if I aint paid!"

Newman looked towards Iona.

"You will be paid right enough and here's the lady as'll pay you, as she's promised."

Mrs. Barley looked questioningly at Iona, who said,

"I love cooking but I hate doing the washing-up. If you will help me, I will pay you three shillings an hour."

It was the amount she knew that the scullions were paid at home and she hoped that it was enough.

There was no doubt that Mrs. Barley's eyes lit up at the idea of three shillings an hour.

"I'll be real glad to 'ave that when things be so bad at the moment with my 'usband and two sons 'avin' little or nothin' to do."

Mrs. Barley was now taking off her hat and coat and it was obvious that she had been in the kitchen before as she found herself an apron out of one of the drawers.

Then, as Iona was thanking her for coming to help her, Newman came in to say that the Earl wanted her.

"He's finishin' his breakfast and I thinks he wants to show you the house, miss." he said.

"That is exactly what I want to see," Iona replied.

She took off her apron and threw it over a chair.

She found it exciting to see this strange house that had been a haven for her when she had been so desperate to find somewhere to stay.

She walked along the passage to the dining room and found the Earl rising from the table having consumed practically everything that she had sent him.

"Good morning, Miss Lang" he said. "I have been wondering since I came downstairs if you had disappeared in the same way you appeared so mysteriously yesterday."

He smiled at her and then continued,

"I came to the conclusion, until I saw my breakfast, that I could not expect to be lucky for two days running."

"I am glad you enjoyed your breakfast, my Lord."

"Of course I enjoyed it. It was straight from Paris. I knew, as soon as I saw the *croissants*."

He laughed as he added,

"How could you look as you do and cook so well? You are a chef straight from the *Rue de Rivoli*."

"I am hoping I shall see a little more of the house before I go back to work in the kitchen," Iona smiled.

"That is exactly what I want you to see. Then you will understand why I behave in such an extraordinary way and never, in my whole life, have I felt so frustrated."

For the moment there was a note in his voice that she had not heard before and Iona said quickly,

"Don't forget that I am sure you will be lucky and you must not despair or upset yourself too quickly."

"That is easier said than done," he replied. "Now come on! I will take you round the house and, if anyone can make my fortune spring out of the bricks, it will, I am quite certain, be you!"

"We shall just have to hope, my Lord, and pray that we will be successful."

The Earl looked at her for a moment and asked,

"Have you already prayed that I might find what I am seeking?"

"Of course I have," Iona replied. "No one could come to this beautiful house or see how lovely the gardens are, as I saw this morning, without thinking that it should be in perfect condition and not allowed to become – "

She stopped suddenly.

She felt that it was wrong to say how she could see already the state it was in because it was so neglected.

Last night she had noticed dust in the dining room, but now that they were in the long passage that led to the hall, she was horrified at the dirt everywhere.

The windows were grubby and not as easy to see through as they should have been.

In the hall she could see that the ashes had not been removed from the fireplace and the windows on either side of the front door were almost darkened by grime.

She said nothing and they walked on until the Earl opened a door of what she guessed was the drawing room.

It was a beautiful room and the furniture in it was all antique and, she knew, very valuable.

The pictures hanging on the walls were by famous artists, but the drawing room was not only dusty but there were cobwebs climbing from one picture to another.

Iona looked round wondering what she should say.

The Earl now said sharply,

"My uncle closed this room up because he was too mean to entertain and it has been allowed to rot now for nearly ten years."

He turned round as if he could hardly bear to look at it and went back into the passage.

When Iona joined him, he slammed the door shut and they walked on.

Every room they entered was in the same state.

The collection of books in the library were thick with cobwebs with large spiders climbing over them.

The music room was in very much the same state and, although she just longed to play the piano, she was sure that it would need tuning.

Neither of them said very much as they went from room to room.

Then he took her up the wide staircase and along a passage to the Picture Gallery.

It was a very large room and the pictures in it were undoubtedly magnificent and worth a great deal of money. It was appalling to think that they had been so neglected.

Every picture wanted cleaning and the floor itself would have been a disgrace to any housemaid.

There was a very fine fireplace at the end of the Picture Gallery and Iona saw in front of the mantelpiece that there was a strange gold cornet.

It was larger and of a different design than any she had seen before.

It was attached to the front of the fireplace which in Mediaeval fashion sloped back so that anyone could walk behind the fire.

She was standing gazing at it and, because neither she nor the Earl had spoken for some time, she remarked,

"That is a strange cornet. In fact I was wondering where it came from."

"One of my ancestors brought it back from Tibet," the Earl replied. "My uncle placed it there for protection for this room, which, of course, is the most valuable in the whole house."

"For protection?" Iona questioned.

"It makes the most extraordinarily loud noise when one blows it," the Earl explained, "and he attached to the chimney above a device that will increase the noise if one blows up through it."

"It sounds very unusual," Iona said. "Why should one want to blow it?"

"Because my uncle believed that, if a burglar was caught trying to steal one of these priceless pictures, those who found him could blow the cornet up the chimney.

"I am told the noise it makes can be heard by the villagers who would then, he thought, come to capture the burglar or any intruder in the house."

"What an extraordinary idea and at the same time it is an original way of attracting attention," Iona laughed.

"My uncle did not encourage people to visit, so I am quite certain if they heard the noise of the cornet being carried to them in the night, they would know something was amiss and come running to either arrest the burglars or support those who were fighting against them."

He gave a little grunt, as he added,

"I say 'those', but until you arrived there was only myself and Newman and his old wife to protect the whole house. I cannot believe that we would be very successful."

"You sound as if you are expecting a whole army of burglars," Iona said. "If you close all the doors, I cannot believe it would be easy to get in or to take away any of these beautiful pictures."

"That is what I tell myself," the Earl replied. "But my uncle had other ideas, although I think the village have long since given up expecting to hear the trumpet call."

He made it sound so amusing that Iona laughed.

"It would indeed need an army of burglars to carry away any of these beautiful but very large pictures, so I am sure you need not be worried about robbers, although, of course, there are many people in every part of the world who would be thrilled to own even one of these pictures."

"Which are rotting as you can easily see, because it is impossible to take care of them. How could my uncle have been such a fool as to hide his money so that I cannot even afford to clean the pictures?"

He spoke so bitterly that for a moment Iona could not think of a reply and then she said in a small voice,

"Are you sure, my Lord, it is not possible for you to sell just one picture to save and protect all the others?"

"Do you suppose I have not thought of that? Of course I have! But those who have been put in the position of guarding the contents of the house and making sure that nothing entailed is sold or stolen, come here once a month to check that I have not broken the law."

"I think that is almost an insult," Iona said, "after all they should take your word for it."

The Earl laughed scornfully.

"They would not trust me with a single miniature, let alone the huge paintings you see here. In fact they are so insulting in the way they check everything, as if I am a common thief, that I always go out when they arrive and stay in the woods until they have left."

"I don't blame you, my Lord, I would do so myself. But then you must find your uncle's fortune, so it will not be necessary for them to come prying on you so often."

"That is exactly what I thought myself, but, as he has hidden his fortune, I believe the only way we can find it is to take down the house and search amongst the ruins!"

"That is something you must not do, my Lord. "It is the most beautiful house. And I have never seen such glorious pictures and furniture as you have here."

"I appreciate what you are saying," the Earl replied, "but you can see the condition everything is in and I often wonder how long I can stay without starving to death."

He did not wait for her to answer, but moved away as if even to look at the pictures in the Gallery upset him.

He then took her down to the guardroom which had been built underneath the house, where there was a superb collection of ancient armour.

There were also strange swords and articles of war from other countries and Iona found them all intriguing.

She kept thinking how thrilled people would be at seeing this amazing collection.

She thought it pitiful that no one would come to the house as it was at present, nor would the Earl want to show the desolation he lived in to strangers.

She was very interested in a small pistol that one of the Earl's ancestors had brought from Russia, which was beautifully set with opals and other stones.

The Earl told her how one of his relatives had used it in a duel and been the easy winner against his opponent.

"It is certainly unique," Iona said, "and I would like to try it out. Do let's fire it in the garden. I am sure you have a target hidden somewhere."

The Earl laughed.

"Of course I have. I will show you tomorrow how accurate it can be despite its age. In case I forget, you keep the pistol and I will find the target."

He put several bullets into a bag and handed it and the pistol to Iona and then they walked upstairs

"There is really nothing more to see except rooms that have collapsed completely," he said, "and so I have merely locked the door and never entered them."

With difficulty Iona bit back words she was about to say and, as if he had read her thoughts, the Earl added,

"Yes, I searched each room before I closed it up, but there was no sign of anything hidden in the floor, the ceiling or the walls."

Again there was bitterness in his voice and it made her feel as if she had made a *faux pas* in even thinking that he had not searched every room thoroughly.

Then the Earl said,

"I suggest we go to the stables. At least the horses are being looked after and the only way I can find enough money to feed them is by selling the horses themselves and a few vegetables from the kitchen garden."

He stopped and shook his head despairingly,

"The one old gardener, who I cannot afford to pay, grows just enough for himself and me."

Again there was a bitterness in his words and Iona did not answer.

She walked beside him as they left the house and walked to the stables, which were large and well built.

There were only four horses left and the long row of empty stalls was depressing.

The Earl, however, was very interested in the two ponies that Iona had brought with her.

"They are an excellent match," he commented.

"They are really meant to be a four-in-hand," she replied without thinking and wished she had said nothing.

"If you own ponies like these," the Earl said, "and have a similar pair, why are you cooking for a living and why are you here in my house?"

"They are questions I do *not* wish, at the moment, to answer, my Lord. You will just have to believe that I was sent to you as a gift from Heaven to cheer you up – "

She smiled at him before she continued,

"Or to tell you in some way or other, perhaps when you least expect it, that you will find the treasure you seek and everything will change overnight."

"Do you think I really believe that?" the Earl asked.

"Of course you do. I am quite certain that you will find it and that everything will be magically different."

He looked down the row of empty stalls and said,

"It was agony to sell my horses. They were mine, not my uncle's. He had already disposed of all his because he had no wish to feed them."

"I have often wondered," Iona replied, "what turns an ordinary man, like your uncle must have been when he was young, into someone so strange and who is against the whole world he lives in."

"My uncle," the Earl answered, "because he was of importance, was forced into marrying a woman chosen for him by his parents. They quarrelled and then she left him, taking a very large sum of money with her. I think he must have hated her and been determined that she would never take another penny from him."

"So that is why he became a miser!" she exclaimed. "I suppose, in a way, I can understand it."

"So can I," the Earl said. "But he is destroying me instead of destroying his wife!"

Iona looked up at him.

She had been thinking ever since she had joined him, how good-looking he was and how tall and slim.

Now she said,

"I cannot believe that you are flunking the jumps that lie ahead of you. Of course, although you don't say so, I am certain that you are determined to win the race."

"How do you know I think that way?" he asked.

"I knew it when you patted my ponies and showed me your own horses. A man who races to win never loses the last and the most valuable race."

"When you talk like that you give me some hope, but to be honest I have almost given up. I have spent every penny of my own and unless I want to starve if I do leave here, I will have to find myself work of some description for which I am paid."

He almost spat out the words and then, much to his surprise, Iona laughed.

"You are already giving up far too easily, my Lord. Of course you will win. Of course you will find what you are seeking."

The Earl did not answer and she carried on,

"I cannot help thinking that you have just gone on blindly looking and digging, rather than thinking it is all a challenge in your mind and being absolutely certain it is not hidden anywhere in the house."

He still did not answer her. He merely looked up at the chimneys of the house silhouetted against the sky.

Then Iona asked,

"Do you really believe that you will fail and leave everything as beautiful and as magnificent as this house to rot until it falls to the ground? You have to win, my Lord, you have to! And that is what you *will* do."

She spoke so positively that the Earl turned to look at her in astonishment.

"Very well, I will believe and if you are right I will win the battle and, of course, make sure that I have done so because you believed in me when everyone else thought I was a silly fool."

"That is one thing I am sure you will never be!" Iona exclaimed. "But you have to fight not only with your strength but also with your imagination and your brain and that is what will make you a conqueror."

"Thank you!" the Earl sighed.

Then, as if he could not bear it anymore, he walked out of the stables and stood looking up at the chimneys.

He looked so strong and handsome in the sunshine.

'He must win,' Iona said to herself. 'If there is any justice in this world or in Heaven, it is only right that he should do.'

Then, almost as if the words came to her lips, she found herself praying,

'Please, please God help him!'

They went down to the lake and Iona asked once again if there were any fish to be found in it.

The Earl assured her there were and suggested that, if she was a fisher, they would spend the afternoon fishing.

"It sounds a fascinating idea, my Lord, but unless you want to go hungry for luncheon, I must soon go back to the kitchen."

"You are posing a difficult choice between being with you and eating the delicious food you cook for me,"

"If we are clever you can have both," Iona laughed. "But I think I should go now to find out what is available or send someone to the village for all I require."

There was silence for a moment and then the Earl said in a hard voice,

"You know I have no money to pay for anything you need to buy."

"I have been told that quite clearly and I promise I will not ask for anything you cannot afford."

"Do you realise what it can be like to be without a penny?" the Earl asked. "There are people working for me who are going home empty-handed and hating me because they think I am the miser and not my uncle."

"That is untrue, my Lord. They do understand the position you are in and I am certain they are all praying that you will find the treasure and make everything right."

"I thought like that when I first took over," the Earl said. "But I have learnt the hard way that you cannot buy what you want without any money and money just does not drop down from the sky."

He was speaking bitterly again and then Iona said,

"Now you go and see about the rods for us to catch the fish with. I will then make the most delicious dish you have ever tasted for dinner. I will go to the house now to see what there is for us to eat for luncheon."

She started off and the Earl joined her.

When they reached the hall, he went below as she expected, because some of the rods she had noticed were in the gun room.

She ran to the kitchen where she found Mrs. Barley talking to Newman.

"I were wonderin' if you'd be back, miss," he said, "as we don't know what you were plannin' for luncheon and then for dinner tonight."

"I will make a list of what we need from the village but you are not to tell his Lordship we are buying anything. He has to believe it is coming from the farm and therefore does not require money."

Newman looked at her.

"Oh, his Lordship be in one of his moods, is he? I thought he'd been too happy ever since you arrived and it wouldn't last."

"He is perfectly happy," Iona said a little sharply. "We are going fishing later and I have a very good dish I can make with the sort of fish that are in these streams."

She sat down at the table and wrote down what she required.

"Mrs. Barley is goin' home," Newman said, "but she'll send one of her sons back with anythin' you require and she is comin' back for the washin'-up this afternoon."

Iona turned to Mrs. Barley,

"That is very kind of you. I think it would be only right if I gave you some money in advance just in case you have something to buy before the end of the week."

She gave her three days' pay and Mrs. Barley was thrilled.

"I never expected this much, miss. I'll be honest and tell you I says to meself if I get a shillin' or two it'll be better than nothin', but this be really worth havin'."

"I am so glad you approve," Iona replied. "At the same time it is best to say nothing in the village or they will all come trooping up here and we will have too many helpers and I will not be able to afford them all."

She had asked for a few items she rather doubted if Mr. Hopkins would be able to supply, but she thought he could be clever enough to send to the next town for them.

They would therefore be available tomorrow or the next day.

Even as she thought about it, she wondered if she would still be here.

Then she told herself that she would be very stupid if she moved.

After she had handed the list to Mrs. Barley and told her to tell Mr. Hopkins that the money would be sent as soon as the goods had arrived, she began thinking about what a commotion there must be at home at this moment.

It had been arranged for her to be married after luncheon as this would give those coming from London time to reach the house and have something to eat before they went to the Church.

'At this moment,' she thought, 'I should be wearing that beautiful white gown I bought in London, my Mama's tiara and carrying a large bouquet of white lilies.'

For the moment she had forgotten the commotion there would be when her relations found out that she had disappeared.

She only hoped that John would be very careful in what he said and did not promise, as they would try to make him do, to find her and bring her back to marry him even though she had upset everything by vanishing.

'How could I have known? How could I have ever guessed for one single moment that he would be in love with someone else and was going to marry me only for my money?' Iona asked herself.

Because it hurt even to think about it, she tried to dismiss the issue from her mind, but she knew that it was still there.

'Whatever happens,' she decided, 'I must not return back until they have all got over the shock of it. John will have to explain why, although we have not quarrelled, I have left him.'

She wondered why she had never been suspicious before that John was in love with someone else.

She had been foolish enough to believe every word he said and it was only by luck that she had been saved at the last moment from marrying a man who was not in love with her.

'If I marry anyone,' she mused, 'it will be because I am absolutely certain he does not love me for my money.'

Even so she felt as if someone was laughing at her for asking too much and she realised that anyone as rich as herself was every man's dream.

She was aware that she was very pretty and being pretty and rich should be enough for any man.

But extraordinary as it seemed, John had preferred Mary and, because neither of them had any money, they would be unable to marry.

'Just how could he do it? How could he make me believe that I was the only one who mattered in his life?' she questioned. 'When all the time he was wanting Mary and she was wanting him.'

For the first time since she had run away, Iona felt as if she must cry.

Then she thought she would not stoop to feeling sorry for herself because she had not been clever enough to sense real love from a man and had been deceived into accepting second best.

'I have been a fool and it is something that will never happen to me again,' she determined.

Equally she was well aware that it would be very difficult when she went back.

Her family probably thought that she would make it up with John and be feeling contrite that she had upset him and everyone else by leaving the night before the wedding.

"Surely," they would say, "John is more important than an old Governess you have not seen for years."

Perhaps as time went by and she was not so close to John as she had been before, they would guess the truth.

'I will have to be very astute about this,' she said to herself.

Equally she felt that she was behaving stupidly.

After what she had said to the Earl this morning, she was not using her brain as she had told him to use his.

'At least I am making one person happy by feeding him the right food,' she thought. 'And I have somewhere to hide where no one is likely to find me.'

These two things were somehow comforting.

As she went back to her room to tidy herself before she started cooking, she thought that the Gods had been very kind in bringing her to this haven where no one could track her down.

For the moment at any rate, she was not missing John or her own home because she had so much to do and so many other issues to think about.

'I will no longer fuss about myself,' she told her reflection in the mirror. 'I will just enjoy being here, then perhaps, if I find the money the Earl is seeking, I will go home, face the music and make it very clear to the family that whatever they may say I have no intention of marrying John.'

As she looked at herself in the mirror, she thought, without being conceited, how pretty she was.

How strange it was that the only man she had ever thought of marrying should love someone else.

Mary was pretty, but Iona knew if she was honest, that she herself was much prettier. Her glorious golden hair would attract any man.

'Perhaps I will never find anyone who will love me for myself,' she thought. 'After all he lived next door and would have been very helpful in running the estate.'

Then she thought a little bitterly that he had thrown her over in loving Mary and the sooner she forgot about him the better.

'After all I have so much here to interest and amuse me,' she thought. 'It is certainly different from anything I have ever done before.'

Then she remembered the number of servants she had employed not only in the country but in London.

She thought it amazing that she had managed to settle in very comfortably when there was no lady's maid to attend to her personally and she was having to cook her own food otherwise she would go hungry.

'The whole scenario is a joke and, if I was clever enough, I would write a play about it and make a fortune!'

Then at the mere idea of money she was thinking again of the Earl and how horrifying his position was.

She could hardly bear to think of the dust and dirt there was everywhere and all the glorious paintings in the Picture Gallery that needed cleaning and restoring.

She thought of the larder next to the kitchen that was empty when it should have been filled to the brim with the delicious goods from the estate.

'I expect,' she said to herself, 'it is very good for me to realise what other people suffer and how the poor live from hand to mouth.'

Then she recalled the huge fortune she possessed in the bank. It was growing larger because of the dividends that came from the money that her father had invested for her all over the world.

She then wondered if love was more important than money or money more important than love.

'I have money and I want love,' she said to herself. 'The poor Earl has nothing except this tumbledown house and John will now have the girl he has always loved more than he loves me.'

It all seemed a terrible tangle and she could not see a clear way to happiness.

But it was so difficult to find a way out even with using her brain in the way she had always been taught to use it.

CHAPTER SIX

Iona and the Earl caught a few very small fish when they went fishing, but they were hardly worth cooking.

They laughed a lot and Iona thought that the Earl looked happier and less worried that he had been since she arrived.

It was growing late into the afternoon when Mrs. Barley arrived with a parcel of groceries she had ordered and Iona saw her name on a piece of newspaper used to wrap up some sausages.

She quickly cut the piece from the package and as soon as she could she went up to her bedroom to read it.

It was what she had anticipated, but it did give her rather a shock to read,

"A consternation took place yesterday at Langdale Hall when the marriage which had been arranged between The Honourable Iona Langdale and Sir John Moreton had to be postponed.

A large number of guests arrived from London and other parts of the County to find Miss Langdale's relations explaining to them that the bride had gone to be with her elderly Governess who was on the point of dying and had asked particularly to see her.

'She felt it was impossible to say 'no', one of her relations said, 'and it was very kind of her to want to be with the old woman who had taught her at least nine years ago before she went to a school.'

No one seemed to know where the old Governess lived, but they were confident that the marriage would be rearranged for the end of the week or perhaps the week after.

Miss Iona Langdale was one of the most successful debutantes of the Season a year ago when her father gave a grand ball for her at their house in Park Lane.

When she had been in mourning, everyone agreed that she was one of the most attractive as well as the richest young girl at all the Season's events and was expected to host a ball this year in Ascot Week.

Sir John, the thwarted bridegroom, was being very brave at the Reception at which the bride was a noticeable absentee.

'I am sure that my fiancée will be returning as soon as she can,' he said, 'but, of course, she may wish to stay until her late Governess's funeral before we can announce our marriage for the second time.'

The most disappointed guests at the wedding party were the children who lived in the village and who had been promised fireworks when the bride and bridegroom departed for their honeymoon.

Nevertheless the fireworks will keep and they will doubtless be flying in the sky when the marriage is actually performed."

Iona read the newspaper twice and looked at the rather bad photograph of herself that had been taken on a Racecourse.

Then she knew that it would be a great mistake for anyone in the house to read it, even though they might not associate her with the lost bride.

She therefore burnt the newspaper and hoped that the same story did not appear in other London newspapers.

'It would be most unhelpful for anyone to find out who I am,' she thought, 'as they might then think it their business to communicate with my family or with John.'

When she thought of him, she did not exactly feel unhappy because she had lost him, but rather upset that she had been deceived into believing he really loved her and was not influenced by her riches.

They had so often talked over what they would do together and the places they would visit and she had felt that it would be fantastic to see the world with him.

Now she was in the position of either having to find another husband or become an old maid at The Hall and have to content herself with looking after the children of her pushy relations rather than her own.

Then she remembered that the world was still at her feet and that she must try and enjoy herself despite all that had happened and somehow find someone she really liked to travel with.

'I will never fall in love again,' she now told herself firmly, 'unless I am absolutely and completely sure that the man in question does not need my money more than he needs me. In fact I will not even give him a second glance unless he is a millionaire!'

Then she laughed at herself.

There really was no use being too serious about it.

She was wise enough to realise that she was very lucky at having found out before she was married that John was in love with Mary, rather than when the ring was on her finger and there was no possible chance of her walking away from what promised to be a most unhappy marriage.

Because she did not want to think of John or The Hall, she concentrated on cooking the most inviting dishes for the Earl, thinking that her father's French chef would be intensely proud of her.

However, because she did not want anyone in the house to find out who she was, she carefully scrutinised every newspaper as it was delivered to The Court.

She was well aware that Newman and his wife were delighted that she was there, not just because she paid them but because they had never known their employer to be in such a good temper.

"He just hasn't yelled at anyone since you've been here," Newman said, "and, as it always upsets the Missus, you can be sure I'm hopin' you'll stay and not go rushin' off with that pair of fancy ponies you brought with you."

"I have no plans to leave at the moment," Iona told him. "I enjoy cooking for his Lordship just as much as he enjoys eating what I have cooked for him."

"There be no doubt about that," Newman replied. "And he looks a lot better than he did when you arrived."

He lowered his voice before he added,

"Of course he's no idea you be payin' for the things as comes from the village. I've told Mr. Hopkins and my Missus to be careful what they says in front of him."

"I don't like to think that I am deceiving him, but I know he would be upset if he found that I was spending my own money when he ought to be paying me for being his cook."

"We can only hope that things run as smoothly as they be doin' since you've come here," Newman remarked. "And the Missus is beginning to look her old self. She's even laughin' which I've not heard her do for months."

Iona thought that they were the nicest couple she had ever come across.

Somehow, when she did leave here, she must try to provide them with some money or they would be down and depressed again as they had been when she first arrived.

*

The next day the Earl wanted her to ride with him.

After they had inspected her ponies, he suggested, as they were obviously so much better than his, that they should ride them.

"I think that we ought to give yours a chance," Iona said. "Your groom was complaining to me only yesterday they were not having enough exercise."

"Very well," the Earl replied. "But we must not neglect yours as they are such a delightful pair."

Iona, thinking he would go on to say how valuable they were, changed the subject, hoping he would forget about her ponies when he was busy with his own horses.

They rode into the woods and inspected the farms.

"I thought of searching the farms and woods for my uncle's money," the Earl said, "but I was almost sure he would not go far away with his spoils."

He laughed as he went on,

"I have always been told that misers like to keep their money within their grasp. In fact, I was told of one man who slept on his money and another who hung it from the ceiling in a bag, so that he could keep his eye on it!"

"I prefer your chandeliers to that," Iona smiled.

"It is what I thought myself, but you do realise that while I am out enjoying myself with you, I have to go on searching for the fortune my uncle has hidden somewhere."

"I still think that if it is anywhere it would be in the house," Iona said. "I feel sure you will find it eventually and it's silly to upset yourself every time you fail."

She felt rather brave in saying this, but she recalled how upset everyone was before she arrived.

"You are making me feel ashamed of myself," the Earl said. "But there is nothing more frustrating than to have one's hopes raised when one was almost certain one was in at the kill."

"You must look on it as a game," Iona suggested, "a game that you can enjoy because it is so stimulating."

"You certainly encourage me, Miss Lang, and now, as I wish to assert myself, I will race you to that wood."

He won easily and Iona recognised that he was a skilled horseman and her father would have admired him.

Newman was waiting for them when they returned to the house.

When the Earl went ahead to take their whips to the cloakroom where they were kept, he turned to Iona,

"There be some strange people in the village, I'm told, wantin' to know who you were and what you be doin' up here at The Court."

Iona was still.

"I-I hope no one – told them," she stammered.

"They asked Mr. Hopkins, but he told them to mind their own business, but I thinks I ought to tell you. Mr. Hopkins thinks they were relieved you were at The Court."

Iona felt herself shiver.

If this meant that the family had found out where she was, they would instantly insist that she went home.

They would be horrified that she was staying with the Earl of Woodbridge unchaperoned and acting, for some reason they would never understand, the part of a servant.

Yet it seemed strange that they had found out where she had gone and anyway she could scarcely believe that John would have encouraged them to look for her.

'If they were told that the woman at The Court is the cook to his Lordship, they will certainly not think it is me,' she reflected.

She was however worried.

The Earl praised the dinner she had cooked for him and insisted that she went to the music room afterwards as she had said she was sure that the piano wanted tuning.

"I want to find out if you play as well as you cook," he grinned.

"You are asking too much, my Lord," Iona replied. "One talent is quite enough for one person and, if you force me to play the piano, I will deliberately play badly as I am sure the average cook would do."

"You are not an average cook and I think, when I look at you, you have every talent in the encyclopaedia."

"You are flattering me," she laughed, "but, as it is something I enjoy, please go on!"

Iona played the piano until it was time to go to bed.

"I have enjoyed this evening almost as much as I enjoyed our ride this morning," the Earl told her. "You make me forget my poverty and the fact that the house is falling down on my head."

"It has not fallen yet, my Lord. I promise you that we will find something to keep it standing."

"Are you speaking as a Scot?" the Earl asked.

Iona nodded.

"Yes, I am using 'fey' to tell you what I believe."

"I am beginning to believe it, too," he answered.

As he spoke, he looked into Iona's eyes.

She felt a strange sensation in her breast.

So much so that she turned around and then walked quickly towards the door.

"Goodnight, my Lord," she said. "I am now going to bed to think out something new to cook for you that you have never eaten before."

"I shall lie awake all night wondering what it will be!"

Iona laughed as she ran up the stairs to her room.

She tried not to look at the dust on the cabinets as she passed them, but it was a joy to find that, because Mrs. Newman looked after her room, everything was becoming cleaner and tidier every day.

'I am very lucky,' she thought as she undressed. 'I might well have been going from one ghastly Posting inn to another instead of which I am sleeping as if I was a Queen under a golden canopy.'

Then, as she opened the top drawer of her dressing table to find her hairbrush, she discovered that lying beside it, Mrs. Newman had placed the pistol that had come from the gun room.

It seemed funny to see the two objects there neatly arranged by Mrs. Newman's hand.

Iona took out the pistol and thought that from the way it was made and its beautiful design it could only have come from Russia.

She wondered if it had a history and wished it could talk.

'I want to go to Russia,' she mused, 'and see the lovely Palaces of St. Petersburg.'

Then she told herself that she was being greedy and most people would be very thrilled to see the magnificent paintings in the Picture Gallery here at Woodbridge Court.

She was brushing her hair as her mother had always told her to do when she heard a sound outside the window.

It seemed as if there was something scraping on the ground and she wondered what it could be.

She blew out the candles, walked to the window and drew back the curtains.

Outside the moon was moving slowly up the sky and, although it was too dark to see very clearly, she could see the fountain on the lawn.

Everything seemed very still.

Once again she heard a sound and looked around.

It was then she gave a sudden start for against the window, which she knew was that of the Picture Gallery, there was something dark that she was sure was a ladder.

It had certainly not been there yesterday when she had explored the garden.

It flashed through her mind that the people making those enquiries in the village had not been interested in her personally.

But perhaps they had wanted to know the number of people living at the The Court, who might prevent them from stealing one of the superb and valuable paintings.

'Just what could be a greater treasure,' she thought, 'than the pictures in the Gallery.'

It was then that she saw, although it was difficult to make out anything very clearly, someone moving round the side of the house.

She realised that there were two men and now she was almost certain that they were robbers.

If they had come to take away the treasures of the house, she would have to prevent them from doing so.

She moved back into her room and began to run towards the door.

Then she remembered the pistol in the drawer of her dressing table.

She pulled it open quickly and took it out.

She saw that the pistol was loaded and did not wait, but held it in one hand as she opened the bedroom door.

She intended to rush down the passage to the Earl.

Then another idea came to her.

If she was able to reach the Picture Gallery before the robbers came through the window, she could blow the cornet the Earl had shown her and the noise would notify the village that the robbers were here and come to help.

She ran down to the lower floor and then along the passage to the Gallery.

She had not put on her bedroom slippers and her bare feet made no sound on the carpet.

She opened the door of the Gallery very gently.

Then she realised that, although the men might be outside, they had not yet been able to force their way in.

It was a blessing that the fireplace was nearer to the door than it was to the window.

She reached it making no sound.

Then, snatching up the cornet, she forced her way over the hearth and crept behind the large fireplace.

As she expected, she would feel with her hands the hole in the wall through which she must blow the cornet to warn the village of the danger that The Court was in.

She had moved so quickly that for the moment she was breathless.

Then she put the cornet to her lips and blew.

The noise it gave out was extraordinary.

It was much louder than she expected and seemed to be multiplied at the top with something she could not see clearly.

The sound seemed to vibrate and vibrate again in the air.

She then felt what she thought were pieces of mud falling down on her shoulders.

She went on blowing until she was out of breath.

Then moving slowly back, she peeped out into the Picture Gallery before she emerged.

To her relief the window was still not open and she guessed that no one had climbed the ladder outside because the noise of the cornet had scared them.

Now she must go and tell the Earl why she had blown the cornet.

She ran through the Gallery and into the passage where it joined the State rooms with the Earl at the end in the Master suite.

She ran towards it and was then aware that the door was open.

She now guessed that the Earl must have heard the sound of the cornet and gone to see what was happening.

She was not mistaken.

When she reached the stairs, she saw the Earl at the bottom and heard the front door being forced open.

While Iona waited at the top of the stairs, two men came in through the door.

She saw that they were roughly dressed and they were carrying heavy iron rods clearly intending to smash open anything that was locked.

"Who are you and what are you doing?" she heard the Earl demand of them angrily.

The men turned towards him obviously surprised at hearing him rather than seeing him in the darkness.

"You have no right to break into my house," the Earl shouted at them furiously.

Without replying the man next to him raised the heavy club he held in his hand and brought it down on the Earl's shoulders.

The Earl then staggered and fell backwards onto the ground.

Iona, without really thinking, but terrified of what they had done to him, raised the pistol, which was still in her hand, and then fired twice at the intruders.

She must have shot one of the intruders through the forehead because he fell instantly backwards onto the floor.

The other man then turned, ran out of the house and disappeared.

It was then that Newman, wearing only his dressing gown over his nightshirt, came running from below stairs, as Iona began to hurry down as quickly as she could.

The Earl was lying on the staircase, his feet on the floor and his body thrown back on the lower stairs.

By the time she reached him, Newman was bending over him and the Earl was absolutely still.

"He hit him," Iona cried, "and he fell directly so he must have hurt him dreadfully."

"His Lordship's unconscious," Newman said. "We must get him up to his bedroom."

Iona looked towards the door, which was open, but there was no sign of anyone outside.

"It was the robbers," she said, "and they were going to climb up a ladder into the Picture Gallery."

"So it's you who blew the cornet," Newman said.

"His Lordship showed me how to do it some days ago," Iona replied, "and I knew it would bring people from the village to help us."

"We'll certainly need them," Newman muttered, looking down at the Earl.

It was, however, so difficult to see anything in the darkness.

"I'll light a candle," Newman said, "and as soon as someone comes we'll get his Lordship up to bed."

Iona was feeling his forehead and gently running her hands down the side of his face.

She could hardly believe that these robbers could have broken their way into the house so easily.

More importantly they had knocked down the Earl almost before she was able to alert anyone to the danger that threatened The Court.

While Newman was lighting the candles, a groom came running in through the open door.

Seeing Iona he asked,

"What's been 'appening? I 'ears the trumpet callin' and came 'ere as fast as I could."

"Robbers have hit his Lordship and he is, I think, unconscious," Iona told him. "Newman wants us to get him back to his bed. Do you think you can carry him?"

"I can certainly 'elp Mr. Newman to do so," the groom answered.

Having lit more candles Newman suggested,

"Let's take his Lordship up the stairs and send for the doctor."

"I'll fetch him in a carriage," the groom offered.

"Let's carry his Lordship to his bed first."

Newman picked up one of the candles and held it over the Earl's head.

Iona saw then that there was blood running down the side of his face and she suspected that the blow had also hit his neck.

She wished that she could do something to help, but Newman and the groom between them managed to carry the Earl along the passage that led to the Master suite.

Left in the hall Iona wondered if she should close the door or wait for anyone from the village to reach them.

It was then that she saw Mrs. Newman come down the stairs, her hair in curlers and wearing a long woollen dressing gown.

"What's happenin'? What be goin' on?" she asked.

"There were robbers trying to steal pictures from the Picture Gallery," Iona replied, "and his Lordship has been wounded and Newman and the groom have taken him upstairs."

"Wounded! His Lordship!" she exclaimed. "I've never heard of such goin's on."

It was then the first men arrived from the village.

"We 'eard the trumpet call," one of them said when he saw Iona, "and we comes to 'elp if we can."

"They were robbers," Iona answered. "They were round the back of the house trying to break into one of the first floor rooms. Please go and see if they are still there and, if they are, arrest them. Then wait for the Police to come and take them away."

Because she spoke is such an authoritative manner, the men obeyed her immediately and disappeared to run round the house to the ladder.

It was not long before other men arrived who had been woken up and were determined not to miss out on any of the excitement.

She told them all what had happened.

While she was still telling them, the men who had been round the back of the house returned.

"The robbers got away," one of them said. "They was travellin' in a fast carriage drawn by two 'orses. We saw it disappearin' down the drive when we comes 'ere and they went by at a great speed."

"Make quite sure they have gone," Iona told them.

The men went round the house only to come back and report that the ladder as still there and a lot of implements to force open the windows.

Because she was so anxious to know how badly the Earl had been wounded, Iona left the villagers with Mrs. Newman and went up the stairs to the Master suite.

The door was open and, when she entered, it was to find that Newman and the groom had put the Earl to bed.

They were now rather clumsily trying to prevent the blood which was running down his cheek and his neck from soiling the white cover of the pillows.

"Let me do that," Iona said, "and I am only hoping the doctor will arrive soon."

"He lives a little way out," Newman volunteered, "but he will have undoubtedly heard the noise you made on that there trumpet and he'll know you needs him."

"If 'e don't come 'ere soon," the groom intervened, "I'll ride over the fields which'll be quicker and tell 'im what's 'appened."

Iona had her hands on the Earl's forehead.

"It was a hard blow," she said. "I am afraid it will be very painful for him when he wakes up. I am worried at him losing so much blood."

"I'll go and fetch some towels," Newman said, "and some bandages if I can find them."

He was gone before Iona was able to thank him.

She just went on mopping up the blood that in spite of her efforts was staining the pillowcase.

She felt it serious that his Lordship was so still and had been knocked out so completely.

She had been so perturbed about the Earl that she had not given a thought to the man she had shot.

He had fallen down beside the front door and had not incurred much interest from Newman or the groom.

When she had seen him, Mrs. Newman had given a scream, but, as he did not move, she paid no more attention to him.

It was, in fact, when the Policeman, who was over fifty and disliked going out at night after he had gone to bed, arrived that the shot robber was attended to.

It was then found that he was dead.

"It's good riddance to bad rubbish," the groom said.

"I agrees with you," Newman responded. "At the same time the Police will want to make a story out of his death and accuse someone of shootin' him."

The groom was listening, but he did not speak.

"What I'll say," Newman added, "is that I fired the pistol. It ain't fair that Miss Lang should be blamed when she only saved his Lordship from worse injuries. She only be a girl and you know how them Police make people feel guilty even when they ain't."

The groom laughed.

"That'll be true enough. Do you remember what a row there was when the old carpenter got shot by mistake and the Police tried to prove that it were part of a vendetta against him."

"I remembers that all right," Newman said. "And this young lady's been kind to me and me wife and I don't want her to get into any trouble."

It was then when Iona joined them in the bedroom that Newman said to her,

"You give me that pistol, Miss Lang, and you say nothin' to the Police about havin' it on you and firin' it."

"I-I think – I killed that – robber," Iona stammered.

"I'm goin' to say I killed him," Newman answered. "It'll be uncomfortable for you, to say the least of it, to be examined by the Police, who'll go on for days takin' down what you've said tryin' to make it into a crime of passion or some nonsense like that."

Iona drew in her breath.

She realised that Newman was absolutely right and, if the Police found out who she was, the newspapers would surely make it into big headlines.

"Are you quite certain that you don't mind telling a lie about it to save me?" she asked.

Newman smiled.

"You've done me and the Missus a real good turn and I'm glad now I can help *you*."

"Oh, it is wonderful of you," Iona told him. "But I will be very frightened in case the Police think I intended to kill him. But I merely fired at him too late to prevent him from injuring the Earl."

"Now you leave all this to me, miss. You just say nothin' except that you blew the cornet to tell everyone in the village that the robbers be attackin' the house."

"I will and thank you, thank you for being so kind."

She thought as she spoke that, if the Earl died of his wounds, there might be a major investigation as to what had happened when the robbers tried to enter the house and that too would doubtless be lapped up by the newspapers.

Iona was incredibly lucky that Newman managed to persuade the Policeman that he had shot from the stairs to protect his employer.

He had only aimed at the robber and had no idea he was such a good shot as to hit him between the eyes.

The Police, as it happened, were far more interested in the Earl. It was obvious from the way they inspected him almost in reverential silence.

The Police were told how the Earl had gone down the staircase to prevent the robbers from entering the house only to be hit so violently with a hard weapon that he could remember nothing when he could see and talk again.

The Police therefore busied themselves with asking questions of Newman, who was well able to hold his own.

When the doctor arrived, he was horrified at seeing what one blow had done to the Earl.

"I cannot send you a nurse," he told Iona, "simply because I don't have one. And, if I had one, it is doubtful if I could spare her for more than an hour or so a day."

He smiled as he added,

"I am sure that you, Miss Lang, and Mrs. Newman will manage and I am also sure that you could get someone from the village to give you a hand."

"Yes, of course," Iona agreed.

The doctor said someone must fetch an ointment from his surgery that was important to help the Earl's skin to heal, as well as the pills and medicines he was to take as soon as he was conscious.

Iona thought that she was so lucky not to be cross-examined by the Police.

'I will reward Newman for this,' she thought to herself, 'and no one deserves it more.'

When she and Newman had carried out the doctor's instructions, it was nearly morning.

It was then for the first time she thought how clever it had been of the Earl's uncle to introduce the cornet call that had brought so many people to their rescue.

If he had not installed it, it would have been quite easy for the robbers to steal his valuable pictures.

But intimidated by the noise and realising that they would be arrested, they had rushed off even before anyone arrived from the village.

The only time that they had been seen was when the first men to reach the drive had to stand on one side to let them pass.

"If we'd known we'd have stopped 'em," more than one man said, "but it's too late now."

Iona thought that they were lucky to have got away.

'I must put the cornet back into its place,' she told herself after she had eaten a little breakfast.

It was not cooked by her because she was busy with the Earl but by Mrs. Newman, who could only do ordinary eggs and bacon which, however, Iona was delighted to eat after a long night of worry and anxiety.

'I will put back the cornet now,' she said to herself, 'and make sure that I have not broken the addition that makes it so noisy at the top.'

She went into the Picture Gallery and thought how fortunate it was that the robbers had not been able to take away any of the magnificent paintings.

'How lucky the Earl is,' she reflected.

Then she remembered that they were not his to sell and perhaps he would never be able to afford to have a son who would inherit them.

She went over to the mantelpiece and put the cornet back where it was meant to go.

Then she thought perhaps it would be a good idea to look up, now it was daylight, and see if the instrument or whatever it was at the top of the chimney was still there.

She recalled that strange objects had fallen on her during the night when she had blown on the cornet and she was worried that, if they were robbed again, its protection might not be so effective.

She climbed round the old chimney.

There was just a faint light emanating from the top, but she saw that there was something on the floor and bent down to pick it up.

Then, as she looked at it in sheer astonishment, she realised that she was holding a golden guinea in her hand.

It seemed for the moment incredible.

She thought that it might well have been dropped in the past by someone like herself who had needed to blow the cornet to attract the attention of the village.

As she looked round, she saw several dark objects that she had thought were dirt or stones only to find when she rubbed them that they too were golden guineas.

It was then looking round the chimney and feeling with her hands, she realised that a number of the bricks had been removed.

Each hole was filled with coins.

When her fingers went back a little further, there was the crackle of banknotes.

For a moment she could hardly believe it was true.

Then, almost as if her whole being was singing, she told herself that she had now solved the Earl's problem and found his fortune.

"I have found it! I have found it!" she cried aloud. "And thank you God for answering my prayers."

At first she felt that she must run down the stairs and tell Newman what she had discovered.

Then she knew it was not her fortune but the Earl's.

It was for him to be the first one to know where it was hidden all these years.

He had tried so hard and been so disappointed time after time that it was wonderful now to know that he was the rich man he had always wanted to be.

The house could now be restored to all its glory.

There was also, Iona thought, as she went back into the Gallery, a fear that Newman might be tempted to keep some of the money for himself.

And Mrs. Newman would find it almost impossible not to relate the exciting story to Mrs. Barley and then it would be all over the village.

It did not require a brilliant brain to know that in which case they could be attacked by so many robbers that they would be unable to defend themselves.

And then the great fortune that the Earl had been searching for could disappear for ever.

'I must keep it a secret as it has been for so long,' Iona decided.

She moved out of the fireplace and made quite sure that it was impossible to see anything unusual if anyone looked at the mantelpiece from inside the Picture Gallery.

All the same it made her run to the Earl's room just in case he was well enough for her to whisper to him what she had found.

But he was still unconscious and Newman said,

"Doctor says he has to find his way back by himself and there's nothin' we can do at the moment to help him. But I don't like it. I don't like it at all."

"You are not saying that he will not recover?" Iona asked anxiously.

"I thinks he will, miss, but he should be comin' round by this time."

He walked away before Iona could say anymore.

*

But, as the day passed, she spent all her time in his Lordship's bedroom.

She kept praying that he would recover and be back to his old self.

He had fought so hard for the fortune that he knew existed and refused to give up his search.

How could he die when it was within his grasp?

When finally late in the evening, the Earl opened his eyes both Iona and Newman hurried to his side.

'He is alive! He is not going to die,' was Iona's first thought.

She bathed his forehead as the doctor had told her to do and made him swallow a liquid to give him strength.

Newman said that he would stay with him all night.

"We will take it in turns," Iona suggested. "I know exactly what the doctor has told you to do and you must be on your guard tomorrow in case people come to see him and upset him in any way."

"You don't think it will be too much for you?" Newman asked.

Iona smiled.

"No, I will be all right. And there is a good dinner waiting for you in the kitchen."

"You're an angel, that's just what you be, miss. If you hadn't come here I really don't know what would have become of me and the Missus. We be so grateful as we always will be for the rest of our lives."

"What we have to do now is to put the Earl back on his feet," Iona said. "So I will stay until one o'clock and then if you take over until breakfast time, we will decide tomorrow how we can arrange the rota better."

"To hear you is to obey, miss, and you've been the kindest person I've ever met and that be the truth."

He went out of the room as he spoke and Iona sat down by the bedside.

"Get well, you must get well," she said to the Earl firmly.

She was not certain if he could hear her, but she felt that if she talked to him she would make him realise how important it was for him to come back to reality.

She carefully rubbed his forehead and then, as the hours passed by, talked to him and wondered if in some magical way he would hear her what she was saying.

She remembered her father telling her once that, if a man had a stroke or was apparently unconscious, he was often aware when people talked to him, especially those he loved, about what was happening even though he could not understand exactly what was being said.

She did not, however, tell him about his fortune.

She talked to him about the land, the house and said how wonderful it would look if one day they could clean the pictures and restore everything to its original beauty.

"If you are proud of it now," she told him, "you would be very very proud if it was as it used to be when you were a child."

She was very sleepy by the time Newman came at one o'clock in the morning to relieve her.

"I've had five hours sleep," he said, "and that's enough for any man as the doctor'll tell you. Now go to bed, miss, and don't worry about his Lordship till the sun is high in the sky tomorrow mornin'."

"I will do exactly as you tell me," Iona said, "and, if you now take my advice, you will sit in that comfortable armchair and put your feet up on the other."

Newman chuckled.

"That's just what I'll do."

Iona took a last look at the Earl and then walked along the passage to her own room.

But, when she climbed into bed and was praying once again that he would soon get well, she knew that in a strange way she had never felt happier than she did at this moment.

She was with people who were so kind to her and people who wanted to help the Earl as she did.

That was all that mattered.

Everything else was of little consequence, even the fact that her family would be wondering how they could find the home of her old Governess.

John would now be, for the moment, keeping up the pretence that he was only postponing their wedding.

'To be honest I am happier here than I have ever been anywhere else,' she thought, 'and I don't suppose I shall ever again have such an unusual adventure as this.'

CHAPTER SEVEN

Iona was preparing a special dish for luncheon and was now wondering if she could persuade the Earl to eat anything when Newman hurried into the kitchen.

"I've just had a man come here from the Police," he said. "They're postponin' all enquiries until Monday."

Iona looked at him in surprise.

"Until Monday!" she exclaimed.

"Yes. After all it's Saturday today and they think that as the robber was dead he'll do nobody no harm in the mortuary. Then I expect that they'll get an Inspector down from London to make the necessary enquiries."

Iona gave a gasp.

"Oh, Newman, then you don't mind saying that you shot him?"

"The Policeman from the village says that he don't think there'll be much fuss about it," Newman answered. "After all, he hit his Lordship first and the doctor will give evidence it were a real nasty blow."

He shook his head before he continued,

"If you hadn't killed the intruder, he might have had another shot at his Lordship and succeeded in killin' him too."

Iona looked horrified.

"Thank God we avoided that and thank you, thank you yet again, for being so kind as to take the blame."

"I'm not sure I'll be a hero," Newman said, "then you'll be sorry you're not in your rightful place."

Iona thought that, if the Inspector came down from London, he might easily have heard of her.

It would be ghastly if it was in the newspapers that the cook to the Earl was a millionairess who had captivated Mayfair with her beauty and her wealth.

She paused for a moment and then said,

"I was thinking just now before you came that if we were wise we would take the pictures out of the Gallery and hide them somewhere where they cannot be seen."

"Why should we do that?" Newman asked.

"Because, when it is known throughout the County that dastardly burglars have tried to break into The Court, undoubtedly there will be many visitors anxious to see the paintings they were trying to steal."

"I sees your point, miss, and it's very clever of you. Of course we'll move the pictures and all they'll see will be an empty room. That'll teach 'em not to go pryin'."

Iona laughed.

"I doubt if it will teach them as much as that, but it will be a wise thing to do and I will help take them down."

"I'll get the gardener to do that. You can trust the old 'un not to talk because he's been here for years. He knows only too well how curious people can be. That's the way he lost some of his best chickens."

"Then I am sure he will help you to keep the nosey parkers away as his Lordship will dislike them intensely."

"What you're cookin' up looks delicious," Newman said. "I'll go and see if there's any chance of his Lordship havin' any of it."

He left before Iona could say anymore and she gave a sigh of relief.

She wanted the Earl to find the treasure for himself and it would be a terrible mistake to have people prying round in case they found it first.

As she went on with her cooking, she knew that she would have to go away.

She had no wish to leave, but with the Inspector coming down, what had happened would undoubtedly be in the London newspapers.

It would only need one person cleverer than the rest to realise that the cook was far too pretty to be there just to do the cooking.

'I must leave here very soon,' she told herself.

At the same time she wanted to stay on as she had never wanted anything in her life so much.

Newman spent the afternoon with the gardener and the groom moving the pictures.

They put them all into a small room near the linen cupboard which no one would think of any interest.

Then Iona locked the door firmly.

"No one'll be interested in that room even if they do go spyin' round the house," Newman told her.

The Picture Gallery now looked most dilapidated indeed.

There were dirty marks on the walls where all the pictures had been, the inevitable dust and a certain amount of rubbish on the floor.

'No one will stop for a moment to look at it,' Iona thought.

Then, as there seemed to be nothing more to do in the house, she went into the garden.

Like everywhere else it looked neglected, but, as the sun was shining and so many flowers were blooming in the flower beds, it was very beautiful.

'I have been so happy here,' she told herself. 'I cannot think why I have to leave.'

Common sense was the answer.

When she took her turn at the Earl's bedside later that evening, she thought that she would be here tonight and perhaps tomorrow night.

Then it would only remain a memory in her mind.

Newman was delighted because he had managed to make the Earl swallow a little warm milk that morning.

He had wanted something stronger, but Iona said it would be a mistake.

"The doctor says he were real pleased with him when he came in this afternoon," Newman remarked. "He says the wound ain't as bad as he thought it were at first."

"I am sure that his Lordship will be back on his feet much quicker than we expected," Iona said. "He is not the sort of man who will want to lie in bed doing nothing."

"That be true," Newman agreed. "He were always on the go even though he did lose his temper when things disappointed him and he found nothin'."

Iona was just longing to tell him that his Lordship would now find all that he was seeking.

But she knew it had to be a secret until he could really enjoy the overwhelming excitement of it at last.

As Newman left her, he said,

"Now you take it easy, miss. If you have a little shut-eye yourself, no one'll blame you."

Iona smiled at him.

"You should go to bed," she told Newman. "You have been on duty all day and must be very tired. Sleep like his Lordship is sleeping as I expect you will have a lot to do on Monday."

"The Policeman in the village says there won't be no trouble about it, because the burglar struck his Lordship first and they has the doctor's report on it."

"As you have said yourself," Iona replied, "I think they should give you a medal as the burglar was obviously dangerous and would doubtless have killed us all if I had not interfered."

"I doubt if I'm as good a shot as you are," Newman replied. "You would win a prize in any competition."

"It's not a competition I would wish to excel in," Iona answered. "But thank you again for your kindness to me which I will never forget."

"Now don't you worry about anythin'," Newman said. "I knows what's right and what's wrong and so does the Police. After Monday I doubt if we will hear any more about it."

Iona wished that this was true and she was still so afraid of the newspapers thinking it a good story, after all any attack on an Earl was worth a front page picture.

When Newman left her, she had one candle burning and was settling herself in a comfortable chair from where she could see the Earl, when unexpectedly he spoke.

"Where – am I?" he asked shakily.

She moved quickly to the bed and, bending down, she said soothingly,

"You are at home and quite safe, my Lord. Go to sleep again and don't worry about anything."

"I am in bed?" he asked. "How did I get – to bed?"

"You have been in bed for some time," she replied, "because you were badly wounded in your shoulder. But it is clearing up and you will soon be on your feet again."

She spoke in a soft quiet voice as she would have spoken to a child.

Then the Earl said,

"Who are – you? Why are you in my – bedroom?"

"You must remember me, my Lord, I am your cook and you are very pleased with the lovely French dishes I prepare for you."

"French dishes? Why – French."

"Because the French have the very best food in the world and that is what you enjoy eating."

There was silence.

Then the Earl opened his eyes as if he was forcing himself to look at her again.

"You are pretty – very pretty," he said and closed his eyes again.

Iona still hovered over him wondering if she should give him anything to drink or whether it would be best to leave him to go back to sleep.

Then she thought that sleep would be for the best and to help him sleep she did what she had done before and massaged the centre of his forehead very very gently.

It had been the one remedy that had helped her mother when she had found it difficult to sleep.

As she touched the softness of his skin and looked down at his hands and face, she realised suddenly that she was in love!

It was a feeling that was different from anything she had ever felt before.

She only knew that she wanted to protect and save the Earl from any pain or stress that troubled him.

Just to be so close to him and to touch him was a wonder that she had never known in her life.

She could not explain it to herself.

But it was something she had never felt for any other man, not even for John, the one she had promised to marry.

Then, as if the very sky opened to her to learn the truth, she realised that this was the love that she had always sought and always wished to find.

The love that was so Holy and there were no words to express it.

Her fingers moved slowly in a circle on the Earl's forehead and she saw that he was now fast asleep.

It was then that she bent forward very gently and touched his cheek with her lips.

"I love you," she whispered. "When I leave here tomorrow, I will never see you again."

She sat near him on the bed all through the hours when previously she had rested in the chair.

She knew that tomorrow night he might be aware of her, in which case she would behave as he expected and not as she wished.

"I love you. I love you!" she wanted to cry out aloud over and over again.

As she knew that she had to go away, she could not prevent the tears from coming into her eyes.

She thought it all out very carefully.

She knew that, when the Earl found the immense fortune he had been seeking, he would feel beholden, as she was to Newman, to give her some of it.

It would be difficult to explain, but, rich though he was, she was very likely richer.

It would be even worse if, when the Inspector came to take a statement from everyone in the house, that anyone here should guess she was not who she pretended to be.

She could imagine all too clearly what a story the newspapers would make of the *debutante* of last Season, one of the richest girls in the country and who had been at every party when she made her debut, was involved in this strange attempt at stealing famous paintings.

They belonged to an Earl who could only afford to have three servants in his vast house and one of them was the beauty of the Season.

'I have to go away,' she thought to herself again as she wiped away the tears running down her cheeks.

She then decided that she would stay with the Earl for the last time on Sunday evening.

*

But on Sunday morning when the doctor arrived to examine him, he announced that the danger was over and all that his Lordship had to do now was to live quietly, eat well and replace the blood he had lost after he was struck down.

"You have done an excellent job," the doctor said to Newman, who on Iona's instructions did not say that he should share the congratulations with the cook.

What he did say, however, before he left was that his Lordship was to eat as much as he could manage and a little light wine would do him no harm.

"It's the best news we've ever had, miss," Newman enthused, when he related the doctor's words to his wife and Iona, who had been waiting in the kitchen.

He looked at Iona as he added,

"I wanted to tell him that I did not deserve all the credit. But I did as you tells me and kept my mouth shut."

"That is just what I wanted you to do," Iona said. "You have been absolutely marvellous and deserve every word of credit the doctor can give you."

"As I said, miss, and I'll tell his Lordship when he's well enough to listen, that you've helped, I thinks, much more than I have."

He took a deep breath before he continued,

"He says to me this mornin' when I were washin' and shavin' him, 'tell Miss Lang I want to see her. I am lookin' forward to having somethin' substantial to eat.' I tells him he'll get that all right!"

He paused before he went on,

"Then he says, 'I expect that you've been stuffin' yourself, in fact, you are a great deal fatter than when I last saw you'."

"That was not an insult," Mrs. Newman said, "it be the truth. We've never had such wonderful dishes to eat as we have since you've been here, miss."

Iona could only smile and then she replied,

"As his Lordship will soon be getting up, I think it would be very nice if we cleaned at least part of the house to celebrate his recovery. Fetch four or five good women from the village to clean some of the rooms and I will pay them whatever you say are the right wages."

"Are you sure you can afford it?" Newman asked.

"Quite sure. I have not forgotten what you have done for me."

He did not ask Iona any further questions.

But later that afternoon, when the women from the village were brushing out the main passages and doing the same to the dining room and to the study where Newman said his Lordship always sat, she went to her own room.

She wrote a short note to the Earl saying,

"The Gods have listened to your prayers and, if you look into the fireplace in the Picture Gallery, you will find behind it all that you have been seeking and, just as good surely comes out of evil, the best thing that could ever have happened was that the robbers should have tried to get in through that window.

I wish you great happiness in the future and in turn I know that you will make a great number of other people happy.

Thank you for your kindness to me which I will always remember.

Ida."

She then wrote another letter to Newman thanking him profusely for all his kindness in taking her place and being resolute enough to persuade the Police that he pulled the trigger and not her.

"*I enclose a sum of money*," she wrote, "*which can never express my real gratitude for what you have done for me. It will, however, make you and Mrs. Newman most comfortable for the coming year.*

I promise it is something that you will receive every year until you are no longer on this earth.

I know you will stay to look after the Earl because he needs you and he would be miserable without you.

But I think it a mistake for you to tell him of my gift to you. I would like it to remain a secret between me, your wife and yourself.

Ida."

She then signed the letter and put in five hundred pounds which she knew would seem an absolute fortune to the Newmans.

She would have given more, but she was frightened of being short of cash herself.

She had already spent quite a lot of what she had brought with her and had no wish to have to go to the bank to draw out any more in case they communicated with her relations.

It did not really matter, but she did not want to take any risks.

When it was time to change places with Newman, she went to the Earl's room, having made preparations for her departure in the morning.

Newman told her in a whisper that he had talked about getting up in a day or so and had eaten an excellent dinner.

"His Lordship's asleep now," he said, "but if he wakes up, there's some hot milk beside his bed and, if he asks for anythin' to eat, I feels sure you'll be able to find him a bite."

He gave a little laugh before he added,

"He ate a big dinner so I thinks he won't be hungry until breakfast."

"I am sure he will not," Iona agreed.

"Are you certain you are not too tired to stay with him?" Newman asked her.

"I can sleep here in the chair," Iona replied. "So you go to bed. You have had a long day and I don't want to have to nurse you as well as his Lordship."

Newman chuckled.

"That'll be the day and I look forward to it!"

"Well, you spend the rest of the night fast asleep," Iona answered, "and God bless you."

Newman smiled at her.

"I think He blessed us all when you came here," he replied. "You made everythin' different and I've a feelin' things are goin' to be good for the future."

"I feel the same," Iona murmured.

He went out, closing the door quietly behind him.

She walked over to the bed and looked down at the sleeping Earl.

'I love you! I love you!' she said in her head. 'If I never see you again, I will never forget you.'

Then, because she wanted his happiness more than anything, she knelt down at the side of the bed.

She prayed that, when he found the money in the Picture Gallery, he would then find the world a very much happier place than it had ever been before.

He would be content because the house could be put back to how it had been in the past and he could fill it with amusing and interesting people without having to then worry about the cost.

As Iona rose from her knees, she realised that the tears were back in her eyes.

Wiping them away almost fiercely, she sat down in the chair that faced the Earl.

Because she wanted to touch him and kiss him, she closed her eyes so that she could no longer look at him.

She told herself that this was a moment she had to forget and she must not now spoil what had been the most thrilling adventure she had ever known.

It was just after five o'clock in the morning and the Earl was sleeping peacefully as Iona crept out of his room.

She left behind on the chair the two letters she had written, one to him and one to Newman.

Then she went up to her room and, collecting the things she had left ready earlier in the day, she carried her cases, with some difficulty because they were heavy, down the backstairs where there was no one to hear her if she tripped or dropped one of them by mistake.

She reached the door at the side of the house that led directly to the stables.

There was only Jeb fast asleep on the straw, where he slept every night.

She crept past him and went to where her ponies were housed, which was some distance from him.

She took them out of their stalls.

She thought that they seemed pleased to see her and guessed that their solitary confinement was over and that they were going home.

Iona too would have liked to go to her home, but she knew only too well that, if she did so, there would be endless questions of where she had been hiding.

Then her family would announce her wedding to John all over again.

She was certain that it was too soon for John to say he wished to marry someone else and they would both be embroiled in the most uncomfortable situation of having to tell lies until her family stopped questioning them.

'I still have to stay away,' Iona told herself, 'and goodness knows where I will go. But it's essential that I don't stay here.'

She fastened her ponies into the cart.

Then she drove off seeing no one and with no one being aware that she had gone.

*

She drove through the village and tried to find the main road that led to the sea.

It was only when she was several miles away and the sun was rising in the sky that she realised she had done what she was afraid would be impossible and left without anyone knowing about her departure.

She was sure that it would not occur to Newman or his wife that she had definitely left and they would expect, if they found her room empty, for her to be in the garden or perhaps down by the lake.

'They will have quite a shock,' she thought. 'But eventually they will forget me, although I will never forget them.'

She drove for quite a long way before she realised that she was feeling hungry.

She stopped in a small village to have some tea and some rather dull sandwiches.

It was in a shop that was clearly patronised mostly, she thought, by children because they sold a very varied selection of sweets.

If anyone was curious who she was and where she was going, they certainly did not ask her any questions.

She then drove on wondering where she would end up, but always aiming towards the sea.

She stopped for a snack luncheon.

Only when it was late in the afternoon did she think that she should now be sensible about finding somewhere to stay the night.

There was no one to ask and she was nervous of going to any of the larger hotels.

She was certain that there might be men there who would behave in the same way as that man had done the first night of her escape from home.

Finally she saw an elderly Parson walking down the road from the Church and drew up beside him.

"I am sorry to bother you," she began, "but can you tell me if there is anywhere I can stay the night where my ponies would be looked after? As I am on my own, you can understand I don't want to go anywhere that I might find uncomfortable because of the other guests."

She spoke shyly, but the Parson understood exactly what she was saying.

"I am afraid that you will find it rather difficult to find the accommodation you require here," he said. "There is, of course, the village inn that is kept by a respectable man and his wife. They occasionally take in a lodger."

"It sounds exactly the sort of place I would like," Iona replied.

"You are really too young to be travelling alone," the Parson remarked. "But I am sure that you will be safe there, especially if you say I directed you to them."

"Thank you, thank you very much, sir."

The Parson paused before he added,

"If you are travelling South, as I expect you are, you will find a charming inn called *The Cherry Orchard*."

He smiled at her before he continued,

"It's only fifteen miles from here, but it's very quiet and respectable and they only take two or three visitors at the inn. They are famous for their excellent food and the majority of people stop there for meals."

"Thank you! Thank you so much," she said. "You are very kind and I am most grateful."

He smiled at her again and took off his hat as she drove on.

She found the local inn and told them that she had been sent there by the Parson.

"Oh, that be the Vicar," the publican said. "He's always been very kind to me and me wife and I'll look after you as he wants us to do."

The food was very poor, but Iona found that there was a good stable for her ponies and her bed was clean and comfortable.

However, she lay awake wondering what on earth she should do when she reached the sea.

If it was possible she wanted to go somewhere safe where she could stay for at the very least three or four months before she dared to return home.

'If only I could have stayed on at The Court,' she thought miserably. 'But they would have discovered who

I was and then I would have to go back and face the whole family demanding explanations from me.'

She was quite certain by this time that someone would have found out that the Governess who had taught her so many years ago was dead.

The one thing she did not want was a hue and cry because she had run away before her wedding

She was quite certain that her whole family would not only be demanding a full explanation for her behaviour but would insist that the marriage, which had only been postponed, should now take place at once.

'I must find somewhere where no one will find me,' she told herself, but had no idea where it could be.

*

The next morning almost as if she was afraid that the Police were not far behind her, she set off very early for the place the Vicar had suggested.

Because the roads were narrow it was impossible to go fast and she did not actually reach *The Cherry Orchard* until it was almost evening.

She could see as soon as she arrived that the garden was as beautiful as the name of the inn.

She learnt from the publican a great deal about the difficulties of accommodating travellers who asked for too much or those who drank too heavily.

"At the same time," Iona commented, "it must be interesting to meet new people. I have never seen anything more beautiful than your garden and the inn itself."

"My wife and I were determined to have somethin' different," the man replied. "We've worked very hard to make this a unique place where people can come and spend their holidays, go to bed early and relax in the garden."

"In other words you don't want people who only stay one night as I am doing," Iona replied.

"I'm hopin' that you'll come back another time," the man retorted. "At least you can tell your friends that this is a home from home."

"I will certainly tell everyone that," Iona assured him. "I can only congratulate you once again on the most beautiful garden I have seen for a long time."

*

When she left the next morning, the publican gave her a bouquet of flowers to take with her and she thanked him profusely.

"I hopes you will come and see us again, miss. My wife is very worried that you are travellin' alone without anyone to look after you."

"Well, tell me where I can stay tonight where I will be as safe and as comfortable as I have been with you."

"I was just hopin' you'd ask me that question," the publican said. "You will find a very nice place in a small village about a mile from the sea. It's called *The Rocking Horse*."

Iona laughed.

"What a funny name!"

"You'll find *The Rocking Horse* very comfortable," the man told her. "They have about eight or ten bedrooms, so you should get in unless you are particularly unlucky."

He paused for a moment before he added,

"If you tell the owner you have come from me, he will do everythin' he can to make you feel at home."

"Thank you very much. I have loved staying with you and hope I can come again."

The publican spread out his hands.

136

"We'll be waitin' for you, miss."

She tipped the ostler generously, who had looked after the ponies, also the servants in the dining room.

As she drove off, the publican waved her goodbye and she thought how kind and understanding he was.

The Rocking Horse was certainly larger than *The Cherry Tree*, but not quite so beautiful.

Undoubtedly the owner of the hotel was determined to make anyone who stayed with him happy and content.

There was, however, to Iona's dismay rather a lot of people already in the reception room. As the majority were men, she felt a little apprehensive.

As she told the proprietor that she had come from his friend, she asked a little tentatively,

"I suppose, as I am alone, it would not be possible for me to have a private room where I can have my dinner. I am, of course, quite willing to pay for one."

The proprietor looked at her and then there was a twinkle in his eyes as he responded,

"I think you are a very wise young lady. Although it is a service we don't provide very often, we have a small room where my wife writes her letters and I add up the bills. We can put that at your disposal."

"That is very kind of you," Iona said.

She thought as she spoke that it was something she was always saying to people.

Perhaps because she was young and alone everyone wanted to help her rather than if she had been older and so could look after herself.

Her room was small but quiet and, when she went downstairs for dinner, she found the small sitting room that belonged to the proprietor and his wife. It was a most delightful little room that opened onto the garden.

She enjoyed her dinner on her own.

Then she was surprised when she was told that the ostler she had left the ponies with wished to speak to her.

She went out into the yard and he told her that one of her ponies had just shed a shoe.

"Oh, dear! I had no idea it was loose," Iona said.

"Well, I can get the blacksmith to call tomorrow," he told her, "but not till the afternoon. I knows that 'e 'as an appointment for a gentleman who 'as large stables."

"I am prepared to wait, if I have to, until tomorrow evening. Will you arrange it for me, please?"

She told the proprietor what had happened and he said,

"We're delighted to have you to stay and, if you are going a long way, I suggest you rest in the garden during the day. Then walk down to the pretty stream where it is cool and I am sure you will be alone."

Iona found that he had not exaggerated.

She then spent the afternoon before the blacksmith came watching the fish moving downstream and keeping in the shade of the trees to avoid the strong sun.

The blacksmith did not arrive until six o'clock, but he quickly fitted a new shoe and patted the pony.

"This be a fine pair you 'as 'ere, ma'am," he said in admiration. "But you mustn't work 'em too 'ard."

"I will try not to," Iona promised. "But I do have quite a long way to go."

She wondered as she spoke if that was true and then she had an impulse to remain where she was.

It would perhaps be better if she stayed by the sea and she would at least be lost in a crowd and so not make people too curious.

She was already aware that both the proprietor and his wife were intrigued to find out why she was travelling alone and it was obvious that a number of their visitors had asked who she was.

'I must move on,' Iona thought. 'Perhaps this will happen to me wherever I go.'

It was impossible when she was driving or sitting alone by the stream not to think of the Earl and how much she loved him.

'Just how could I be such a fool as to have fallen in love for the first time immediately after I had lost John?' she asked herself.

Then she thought that she should be grateful to God that she had not been married to John before she realised that his heart lay elsewhere.

And that he was only marrying her, as so many men had wanted to marry her, for her money.

'At least no one will think that I am very rich now,' she mused.

Yet after her first night she realised the predicament she was in.

'What am I to do?' she prayed. 'What am I to do?'

But there did not seem to be any answer.

Only a blankness that she thought was even more frightening than if she had something definite to be worried about.

She had a bath before dinner and then went down to her quiet little room.

There was a big party in the dining room and she was so glad, when she heard loud voices and laugher, that she was not there.

A pretty woman sitting by herself in a corner was certain to arouse interest.

She knew that she would have been afraid if one of the men, more adventurous than his friends, had introduced himself.

She might have been asked to join the party and it would have been difficult to refuse.

'Whatever can I do?' she asked herself again. 'I cannot go on like this for ever. I dare not go near any of my friends because, however much I may ask them to keep my presence a secret, they would be certain sooner or later to let one of my family know where I was.'

She finished her dinner and was just thinking that she might be wise to go to her room when the door opened.

"There be a gentleman to see you," the proprietor announced.

As he closed the door, Iona turned round.

She had been standing gazing out of the window at the sun sinking behind the trees.

Now she realised that there was a man just inside the door of the small room.

She looked at him.

And then she froze into immobility.

It was *the Earl* standing there!

He was looking extremely handsome. At the same time slightly pale from the ordeal he had been through.

"Oh," she exclaimed tremulously, "it is – you!"

"Yes, it is me," he replied sharply, "and a very nice dance you have led me. How dare you run away just like that without telling me where you were going and why you were leaving!"

He spoke so fiercely to her that she could only stare at him.

Then he asserted,

"I suppose you know that it might have killed me following you all this way! But what else could I do?"

"I don't know why you are here," Iona murmured. "I told you – where to find the treasure – you have been seeking."

"Yes, you told me that, having found for me what I had been seeking for so long and, having saved my life, you could just walk out and leave me as if we were of no consequence to each other."

He walked slowly towards her as he spoke.

Now he stood looking down at her.

"How could you have been so cruel, so utterly and completely brutal in running off like that," he demanded, "and not telling anyone where you were going?"

He was still speaking furiously.

Then in a very small voice Iona told him,

"I had – to go."

"Why? Why should you go? You could not have been frightened of the Police as Newman had told them he killed the man and, as the robber had already assaulted me, there would have been no trouble over what had occurred."

"I am glad – about that," Iona stammered. "It was very kind of him – to take the blame."

"What about *me*? Have I not been kind to you?"

"Yes of course – you have," Iona replied.

It was difficult to speak as she was so overcome at the Earl's appearance and the anger and fury in his voice.

Then, after a long silence, she asked,

"Why are you so angry?"

"Surely you should know the answer to that!" the Earl snapped. "How could I lose you? How could I let you go when you saved my life and found the treasure I thought

I would never find? Did you really think that you could walk out of my life and I would not miss you?"

Iona felt as if her heart turned a somersault.

Then she asked in a small voice,

"Did you really – miss me?"

"I nearly went mad when I heard that you had gone. They kept it from me for the first day and then, when I demanded to see you, they told me the truth that you were no longer there. How could you do it? How could you be so unfeeling and so *cruel*?"

He was still speaking very angrily.

Iona stared at him.

As their eyes met, it was impossible for her to look away.

Slowly, so slowly that she was hardly aware that he was moving, the Earl drew nearer to her.

He put out his arms and pulled her close to him.

"You must have known," he said quietly in a voice that was no longer angry, "that I could not live without you."

She looked up at him.

Then, as he pulled her even closer to him, his lips found hers.

For a moment he kissed her very gently.

Then demandingly and almost angrily as if he was afraid of losing her and punishing her at the same time.

When his lips set her free, she hid her head against his shoulder.

In a voice quite different from the tone he had used before, the Earl said,

"I think even if you did not admit it, you loved me a little. You could not have cared for me or taken so much trouble if you had not done so."

Almost as if the words fell from her lips without her really saying them, Iona whispered,

"I love – you! I love you!"

"And I love you, my darling," he asserted. "If you think I was going to lose you, you are very much mistaken. You are mine and, when I looked at the fortune you had found for me, I knew it was unimportant beside you."

"Are you really – saying this to me?" she stuttered.

"I have much more to say, but for the moment I only want to kiss you and make quite sure I have found you. If you hide from me again, I think I will kill myself."

Iona put her head against his shoulder.

"I thought it would have caused a lot of problems – if I had stayed with you," she whispered.

"There is just one problem for me," he replied, "and that is I might lose you again! We are going to be married immediately and I will make sure that you cannot run away from me this time."

Iona looked at him with tears in her eyes.

"How can you say such – wonderful things to me?" she asked. "And did you really say – you wanted to *marry* me?"

"Of course I want to marry you, but I am frightened to ask the question in case you say 'no'. But I want you, I need you and I am never going to lose you!"

He was then kissing her again.

Kissing her until she felt her body melt into his and they were flying into the sky and touching the stars one by one.

Only when he raised his head did she ask,

"How could you have driven so far? How did you find me?"

The Earl laughed.

"I started off on Monday as soon as the Inspector, who had come down from London, disappeared. Newman told me in a whisper not to mention that you were in the house or had ever been present."

He smiled at her before he continued,

"He had already told me that it was you who had saved my life and that he was to take the blame for the shooting."

As he was speaking, the Earl sat on a small sofa and pulled Iona down beside him.

With his arms round her it was impossible for her to move.

"I followed you, my precious darling, as I knew instinctively that you would go South. I had a feeling that it was the North that intimidated you for some reason."

Iona thought just as she had felt things about him which were fey that he felt the same about her.

"I then followed you from place to place," he said, "after all, a girl as young and as beautiful as you, moving about the country and driving without a groom would be sure to be noticed."

Iona grinned.

"I did not think about that."

"Did you think about me?" the Earl asked.

"Of course – I did."

Even as she spoke, she was thinking how wonderful it was that he loved her.

He did not know who she was or where she came from.

He just loved her because she was herself.

Then, as he knew what she was thinking, he said,

"We have so much to tell each other, but the only issue that really matters is that you love me. I knew it when you talked to me when I was unconscious."

Iona gasped.

"I knew it," the Earl went on, "when you massaged my head and I felt your fingers putting your life force into my body."

"You are not really well enough to travel so far, so quickly," Iona pointed out.

The Earl chuckled.

"I felt you would say that. But you can be certain that I will stay here tonight and tomorrow and then we will be married."

There was a moment's silence.

Then Iona, hiding her face against him, murmured,

"It is not as easy as that."

The Earl stared at her.

"What can you mean by that? You are not already married?"

"Of course not!" she replied. "It is just that I am not who you think I am."

"I know everything about you that I want to know," he told her, "and I love you just as you are. If you commit murder or steal a fortune, it's of no interest to me. What I want is *you*! You are tied to me as my wife for the rest of our lives."

He spoke almost sharply and in a different tone he added,

"I believe, my precious one, that we will be very very happy."

"I know we will," Iona said, "and I think it is the most wonderful thing that has ever happened that you love me for myself, knowing nothing about me."

"I know all I want to know," the Earl repeated. "You are beautiful, you are perfect and you belong to me. There is nothing else that could matter to either of us."

Iona thought of her large family and then she said in a rather small voice,

"If we are to be married – I must tell you – who I am."

"Does it matter? You will take my name and that is what I want you to do. Quite frankly I am not interested in anything else."

Iona laughed simply because it was all so unusual.

She felt that they were riding on a cloud and the world beneath them was, as he had said, of no significance.

She put her head against his shoulder and asked,

"Can this really be happening to me? I was just so miserable at leaving you because I believed that I would never see you again."

"How could you have done anything so cruel?" the Earl said. "When I heard that you had gone, I nearly went mad."

"Did you really think you would find me?"

"I thought, or perhaps you inspired me to think, that you would go South. When I came to the first place where you had stayed, they recognised you as the lady who had come alone and so the publican had taken you to his wife."

"They were very kind, but I was apprehensive."

"Of course you were. Did you really think that you could go about alone, unchaperoned and unprotected?"

"I had to go – away," Iona said again.

"And leave me?" he questioned. "Why should you want to do that unless there is another man in your life?"

Now there was a harshness in his voice and he was staring at her as he had when he had first arrived.

"No! No! There is no one else. At least, I suppose in a way there was, because I promised to marry him and then found out that he loved someone else and was only marrying me for – "

She stopped for a moment before she whispered,

" – my fortune. I am very rich."

The Earl stared at her and then he laughed.

"I don't believe it! How can you be very rich and be working as my cook?"

"It was such a perfect way to hide," Iona replied. "My wedding was planned for the day I ran away."

"Did you love this man?" the Earl enquired.

"Not as I love you," Iona answered truthfully. "In fact I did not know love could be so overwhelming and so different to anything I have ever felt before."

The Earl pulled her closer to him.

"You are mine, mine completely and, my darling, I will teach you about love, the real love that you and I have for each other."

He gave a deep sigh and added,

"That is why I nearly went mad when I found that you had gone and Newman had no idea where you were."

"I ran away because the Police were coming and I thought that the newspapers would take up the story and the fact that, if they discovered that I was your cook when I had run away on the day I was supposed to marry someone else, it would make such a story that it would be headlines in every newspaper."

"Of course it would," the Earl said. "But you have still not told me who you are."

"I don't suppose you would know if I do tell you," Iona replied. "Perhaps you will not want to marry me – "

The Earl laughed and drew her a little closer.

"I want to marry you if you have committed every crime in the book and, even if you are a criminal, I will somehow get you reprieved."

"I am not quite that bad! "But I learnt on the day before I was to be married that the man who was to be my husband was marrying me for my money, but was really in love with someone else who he could not marry because he was so poor."

"So you ran away," the Earl observed.

Iona nodded.

"I came to you because you wanted a cook and I felt that no one would ever find me if I was buried in your kitchen."

"That is certainly true, but I still don't know your name."

"You may well have heard of my father," Iona said, "who was Lord Langdale. He was very important in the Government. My real name is Iona Langdale."

She sighed before she continued,

"When Papa died, he left me an enormous fortune and I have always been afraid that someone would marry me, as John was trying to do, for my money."

"Well, I have no need of your money, Iona. Thanks to you I can spend my own. One thing we have to do is to put the house back as it should be, although I think I hate it for all the misery and unhappiness it has caused me these past years."

"Then I would like you to see my house," Iona answered. "Although I don't have such a fine collection of antiques and pictures as you have, I think you would enjoy the stables and the horses that my father left me."

The Earl laughed.

"I just don't understand this conversation," he said. "Here I have been starving myself for years, living in utter discomfort and misery and now between us we have almost too much to cope with!"

"For *you* to cope with," Iona corrected. "After all I want my husband to run the place, while I just try to look beautiful for him."

The Earl laughed again.

"There will be certainly no difficulty about that and how quickly, my precious Iona, can we be married before anyone tries to snatch you away from me?"

"I don't want anyone to know we are married until we actually are. I could not bear a grand Reception with everyone whispering that I had thrown over John, who is really a very nice man, because I wanted a better title."

"That is just the sort of thing they would say," he said, "and one we must avoid. I had already planned what I would do when I found you and that I will put into action tomorrow long before anyone finds us or even begins to look for us."

"Please explain what you mean?" she begged.

"I thought and I admit it was because I did not want my relations to think that, because you were a cook, you were not good enough for me. So to save any trouble and also to avoid having to obtain a Special Licence that we would be married at sea."

"How could we do that?" Iona asked.

"Very easily now that you have found my fortune for me. I have a good friend who has been pestering me for ages to buy his yacht as he wants a new one. Actually it is extremely comfortable as I found on several journeys abroad with him."

"So we will be married at sea," Iona reiterated. "That is very clever of you."

"We will be married at sea and no one will know we are married until we come back from our honeymoon. As you know, a marriage performed at sea by the Captain of the ship is totally legal. If you want a big Reception when we return, you shall have it."

"I don't want anything – but to be alone with you," Iona whispered.

He held her so tightly that it was almost painful and then she said,

"I am sure that this is all too much for you in one day. If we are to be married tomorrow, then I suggest that you go to bed now in case you collapse and I have to nurse you all over again."

"The doctor said that I was perfectly well as long as I ate plenty of good food and did not exert myself, but you made me exert myself to find you and now you have to look after me and make me strong enough to keep you my prisoner for all Eternity!"

Iona smiled.

"A very willing prisoner. Oh, Michael, I love you so much. It was agony leaving you."

"It was agony for me finding that you had gone and it must never happen again. Just promise me one thing, my darling, that you will never love anyone but me and we will be happy with our children for ever and ever."

He spoke so seriously that Iona replied,

"Of course I promise all those things. Our children will have two enormous homes to enjoy themselves in."

"That is just what you would say and I admire you for saying it. But, my beloved, we will, neither of us, ever be bored. I am certain that everything which matters to us will always be unexpected, will always be an adventure and eventually a happiness that will carry us into a perfect Heaven of our own."

Iona put her arm round his neck.

"How could you say anything so wonderful? It is exactly what I want to hear. I love you, I adore you and, as you say, I know that we will be very happy and it will all be marvellous."

The Earl rose to his feet and pulled her to hers.

"We will go to bed," he said, "and tomorrow we will travel to my friend at Bournemouth and go onto his yacht. He wrote to me a week ago to say it was available if I ever wanted it."

He paused before he went on,

"I thought then I could not even afford the expense of reaching him. Now, with the vast fortune you found for me, the world is ours and we will be married tomorrow as soon as we are at sea. Then my darling, I will teach you about love."

Iona drew in her breath and hid her face against his shoulder.

"It is all too marvellous to be true," she sighed. "I feel so happy I think I must have reached Heaven already."

"I will make you happier still," the Earl promised. "Now, my darling, you need your beauty sleep."

"That is what I should be now saying to you. Oh, Michael, is this really happening or am I dreaming?"

"I will tell you tomorrow morning," he answered.

He took her hand in his and drew her from the little room and up the stairs.

She found that his bedroom was next to hers and she could see a large trunk that Newman must have packed for him.

He took her to the door of her room and kissed her very gently.

"I love you and adore you," he said. "But tonight I know that I have to be well for tomorrow, which will be the most important day of my life. So I am going to bed to dream about you, but tomorrow night will be very very different."

He kissed her again gently.

Then before she realised just what was happening he had gone into his room and closed the door.

She went to her room and saw that the bed had been turned down and her nightgown laid out for her.

Before she began to undress she went down on her knees.

In a prayer that came from the depths of her heart she said,

'Thank you, God! Thank You! I have found him and he has found me and we will be unbelievably happy.'

Then because everything was so wonderful and so perfect, she felt the tears come into her eyes.

Only now they were tears of love.

The Love that comes from God, belongs to God and would be theirs for all Eternity.